## "I'm fine, Cliff." Ruby tossed her purse on the table. "You can leave."

"I will. Soon."

Was it possible he didn't want to go?

It was entirely possible *she* didn't want *him* to go.

"Can I get you something?" She wasn't thinking of water.

Neither was he. Heat flared in his eyes. "I'm okay."

Seconds ticked by. Neither of them moved.

This was stupid, Ruby thought. Any relationship they had was doomed from the start. Her home was in Vegas. His was in Sweetheart, three hours away. She was evading a stalker and would probably be a material witness in his upcoming trial. One of them needed to be the adult.

"I'm pretty sure the coast Is clear," she said.

"You're right." He inched slowly away.

She buried her frustration. What did she expect? For him to sweep her into his arms? Hadn't she just admitted the pointlessness of that?

He hesitated on the porch. "I had a nice time tonight."

Her heart skipped. That was the kind of remark a man made to a woman at the end of a real date. Not a pretend one.

Dear Reader,

I often plot my books many months before I start writing them. In that time, the story outline sits tucked in a file underneath a lot of other files without me looking at it much. When I finally begin writing the book, it can be a little disconcerting. Did I really think this was a good story? Are these characters the least bit appealing?

Once in a while, however, magic happens. That was the case for me with *Most Eligible Sheriff*, particularly with my hero Cliff Dempsey. As the words flowed and the story took shape, he became a different person than I first imagined him to be. Deeper. More complex. More interesting. More troubled. And let's face it—a troubled hero makes for an interesting hero! Oh, and he has this great sidekick. A three-legged retired police dog named Sarge—who was a complete surprise when he suddenly appeared on the pages one day.

Yeah...magic.

While I'm sorry to think about my Sweetheart, Nevada series ending, I thoroughly enjoyed writing this last book. I hope you enjoy reading it, and that Cliff and Ruby's struggle to find love touches your heart as it did mine.

Warmest wishes,

Cathy McDavid

P.S. I always enjoy hearing from readers. Visit me at www.cathymcdavid.com, or you can contact me at cathy@cathymcdavid.com.

# MOST ELIGIBLE SHERIFF

Cathy McDavid

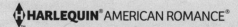

HARLEQUIN® AMERICAN ROMANCE®

Recycling programs
for this product may
not exist in your area.

ISBN-13: 978-0-373-75511-0

MOST ELIGIBLE SHERIFF

Copyright © 2014 by Cathy McDavid

This edition published by arrangement with Harlequin Books S.A.

For questions and comments about the quality of this book, please contact us at CustomerService@Harlequin.com.

Printed in U.S.A.

www.Harlequin.com

## ABOUT THE AUTHOR

Cathy makes her home in Scottsdale, Arizona, near the breathtaking McDowell Mountains, where hawks fly overhead, javelina traipse across her front yard and mountain lions occasionally come calling. She embraced the country life at an early age, acquiring her first horse in eighth grade. Dozens of horses followed through the years, along with mules, an obscenely fat donkey, chickens, ducks, goats and a potbellied pig who had her own swimming pool. Nowadays, two spoiled dogs and two spoiled-er cats round out the McDavid pets. Cathy loves contemporary and historical ranch stories and often incorporates her own experiences into her books.

When not writing, Cathy and her family and friends spend as much time as they can at her cabin in the small town of Young. Of course, she takes her laptop with her on the chance inspiration strikes.

**Books by Cathy McDavid**

To my mother. I don't tell you often enough how greatly you enrich my life and how much I value the lessons you've taught me. Love ya.

# Chapter One

Seriously, who in their right mind hid a spare key under a flowerpot where any thief could find it? Ruby McPhee's sister, apparently. Climbing the porch steps, Ruby counted the third chrysanthemum from the right. The key was there, exactly where Scarlett said it would be.

*Small-town living,* Ruby told herself as she opened the trailer door—only one lock, no dead bolt—with shaking fingers. Inside, she felt less anxious than she had outdoors, but not much.

At the front window, she pushed aside the curtain. Early morning sun cast lengthy shadows across the yard, the exaggerated silhouettes of tall ponderosa pines resembling daggers.

Okay, she was letting her imagination get the best of her. No one, not even her boss at the Century Casino or her closest friends, knew her exact whereabouts. Just her sister and the Las Vegas police detective assigned to her case. The one who had recommended she lie low for a while after her stalker violated the order of protection against him and showed up at her work, looking for Ruby and threatening a coworker.

*Her case. Lie low. Order of protection.* The words had a scary ring to them, and Ruby was tired of being scared. That was the whole reason she'd come to Sweetheart, Nevada, this out-of-the-way little mountain town. To be safe and to sleep through the night undisturbed by sudden noises and bad dreams.

She let the curtain fall back in place and inspected the single-wide trailer. It was old and sparsely furnished with the barest of necessities. So typical of her sister, who rebelled at the thought of lingering too long in one place.

Ruby sighed and started toward the narrow hall leading to the single bedroom. Despite a lack of creature comforts, the trailer would suit her purposes just fine.

Something caught her eye as she passed the worn checkered sofa. A framed picture, the only one in the room, sat on an end table. She picked it up, recognizing the photo as one taken a few years ago at their mother's birthday party. Her heart immediately softened.

Like most identical twins, Ruby and Scarlett were the spitting image of each other. So much so, they were nearly indistinguishable when dressed the same. But unlike most identical twins, they weren't inseparable and didn't share some sort of psychic connection. They'd grown apart during high school and had never quite bridged the gap that widened when their mother remarried.

Until now. Scarlett had come to Ruby's aid when she needed it most. Perhaps blood really was thicker than water after all.

Replacing the picture, she removed her smart phone from her purse, sat on the sagging sofa and dialed her sister's number. Scarlett answered on the first ring. She sounded so happy, Ruby almost forgot her own worries. Almost.

"You made it," Scarlett said. "Any problems?"

"None. Thank you, MapQuest."

"I really, really appreciate this."

"I'm the one who owes you."

"They're going to put that guy away, Rubes. Don't worry about it."

"Right." Ruby shivered at the reminder. How could she not worry?

She saw herself coming home at 3:00 a.m. and walking unsuspectingly into her darkened condo. Heard again the strange scuffling sound, then heavy breathing as an inky figure emerged from behind a corner. Felt strong hands grab her by the throat and squeeze, cutting off her air supply.

Only a miracle had enabled her to escape with minimal injury.

Forcing a calming breath into her lungs, Ruby changed the subject. "Things okay with you and Demitri?"

"Wonderful. Fantastic. It's going to work this time."

"I'm glad."

Scarlett had left Sweetheart for San Diego around midnight. Three hours later Ruby was in her car and leaving the Vegas city limits.

Her sister was meeting her off-and-on-again boyfriend for yet another reconciliation while Ruby was taking her sister's place. Literally. Occupying her trailer and filling in for her at work.

The two sisters had spent the better part of the previous evening on the phone, with Scarlett describing in detail her job, her boss and his wife, their family, the Gold Nugget Ranch where she worked as the only female wrangler, and the layout of the town.

Ruby had asked endless questions and scribbled pages of notes. Still, she worried about her ability to pull off the switch. Especially the job part. While once an accomplished rider, she hadn't been on a horse in eleven years. Hopefully, it was like riding a bike.

"If things go well," Scarlett continued, "and I'm sure they will, I won't need my job anymore."

"Would you be happy living in San Diego? You've always been a country girl."

"I'll be happy anywhere, as long as I'm with Demitri."

Scarlett's boyfriend worked as a marine biologist at Sea-World. Currently, Ruby corrected herself. He traveled extensively and often spent months at sea aboard a research vessel. Well, working in their favor, Scarlett wasn't a homebody. Another distinction between the sisters.

"You'd better hurry," Scarlett said.

Ruby glanced at her watch and mumbled a curse. She—Scarlett—was due at the Gold Nugget in twenty minutes.

"Boots!" she blurted.

"In the bedroom closet. Jeans are in the dresser. Good luck."

"What about—"

"Gotta go, sis. Demitri's leaving. Bye."

With that, Scarlett disconnected, and Ruby was left to manage on her own.

She hit the bathroom first, washing the lack of sufficient sleep from her face and arranging her hair in a simple ponytail. Ruby, assistant manager of the casino's exclusive VIP lounge, wore carefully applied makeup and elegantly styled her long tresses. Scarlett the cowgirl didn't bother with makeup or styling her hair. Too much trouble.

In the bedroom, Ruby ransacked the closet and bureau drawers, finding jeans, a shirt, a belt, socks and boots. As she dressed, she reviewed her pages of notes laid out on the bed.

Scarlett had only worked at the Gold Nugget Ranch for three months. Nowhere near long enough to have earned vacation time. It was also May, the start of the guest ranch's busy season and a month before some huge town-wide wedding event. The ranch couldn't spare her.

That didn't matter to Scarlett, however. If Demitri wanted her to come to San Diego and give their relationship another go, she'd do it and damn the consequences.

When Ruby had told her sister about the stalker and the detective's recommendation that she leave Vegas, Scarlett, always the more daring of the two, proposed that they change places. No one would find Ruby, and Scarlett would have a chance to visit Demitri without losing her job.

Ruby's boss, sympathetic to her plight, had given her the time off, with the promise she return after her attacker's arraignment. While it was doubtful her stalker would plead guilty, it was hoped he'd leave Ruby alone, not wanting to make his case worse by committing another crime.

Crazy as it sounded, the old switching-places scheme might succeed. Ruby and Scarlett had done it before. Frequently, in fact, when they were younger.

Once, Ruby had impersonated Scarlett and taken a difficult calculus test for her during their junior year in high school. Another time, Scarlett had broken up with Ruby's boyfriend when Ruby didn't have the nerve.

This *could* work. Ruby just needed to stay focused and keep her wits about her. Not give anyone cause for suspicion.

She didn't require MapQuest to find the Gold Nugget Ranch. There were plenty of signs in town pointing the way. She read them in between looking anxiously in her rearview mirror or over her shoulder—habits that had become second nature last month when the stalking started, and increased last week after the attack in her condo.

At the gas station where she filled up her car, she paid at the pump, in case someone inside was friends with Scarlett and would want to chat.

Her car! Oh, no. She hadn't thought about that until right this second. Scarlett drove a Jeep. Someone was bound to notice the strange vehicle and ask questions. The three-mile drive along the highway to the ranch gave Ruby time to concoct a plausible story.

A rental car. Because her Jeep was in the shop. Yes, that sounded good. She repeated the fabrication three times over so it would flow more naturally off her tongue.

Perspiration formed on her brow. This leading a double

life wasn't going to be as easy as she'd first thought. Maybe she—Scarlett—should call in sick for the week after all. Scarlett had actually suggested it, but Ruby dismissed the idea, not wanting to give her sister's boss a reason to fire her.

Ruby had her doubts about this rekindled romance with Demitri. If he and her sister broke up again, which was likely given their history, Scarlett would need a job.

When Ruby pulled into the ranch, she drove slowly, visually comparing the buildings and landmarks with those her sister had described. Spotting the barn, she headed straight there and pulled in next to a pickup truck parked along the side. This, Scarlett had advised, was where the wranglers left their vehicles.

Standing outside her car, she paused. The horse corrals were across the way. Beyond them, the arena, bunkhouse and, on the nearby hill, a half-dozen guest cabins. She should head toward the corrals. Scarlett had told Ruby to check in with the trail boss first thing upon arriving.

At the sight of so many people gathered at the corrals, she momentarily lost her nerve and ducked into the barn instead. Just for a few minutes, she told herself. Until she felt calmer.

The smell of hay and horses triggered memories of years gone by when riding had been part of Ruby's daily life. She made her way to the four box stalls standing in a row. According to her sister, the working trail horses were housed in the corrals, and the barn served as a sort of infirmary.

Two stalls were empty. A third contained an old, swaybacked mare and the fourth a pony that poked its nose over the side of the stall and nickered at her. She couldn't resist and reached out to pet the whiskered face.

"How you doing, little fellow?"

In reply, the pony pressed its warm nose into her palm.

"Hey, Scarlett, what's going on?"

Ruby spun, alarm shooting through her in waves, and

faced the woman who had come up silently behind her. Hoping her smile didn't appear too nervous, she tried to place the woman from her sister's descriptions. The owner's wife? In her current disconcerted state, Ruby couldn't remember.

"H-hi. I'm…ah…checking on the pony."

"Mooney's fine." The woman smiled in return. "Her thrush is much better."

Ruby mentally repeated the pony's name and ailment for future reference.

"Lyndsey's been taking care of her," the woman continued. "Cleansing the hoof and medicating it."

Lyndsey? That was one of the owner's little girls. Could this woman be Annie, his wife? Ruby wished she could be sure. She didn't dare call the woman by name for fear she was wrong.

"Well, good," Ruby replied. "I'll just mosey on over to the, ah, corrals, then."

She shoved her hands in her jeans pockets, and then whipped them out, deciding the stance made her look uncomfortable. Which, she was, but she didn't want to appear that way

"Stop at the house first," the woman instructed. "I got a call a minute ago. Someone's here to see you."

"Who?"

There was a twinkle in her eyes. "Who do you think?"

"I don't know."

"Cliff, of course." The twinkle brightened. "He's waiting in the kitchen. Come on, I'll go with you. The first trail ride isn't for another hour. You have plenty of time for a visit."

Time, but no desire. Not until she was more acclimated to her surroundings.

The kitchen, Ruby recalled, was in the main house. Halfway there, she and the woman passed an SUV. She noticed the official logo on the side and came to a sudden stop, the alarm from earlier zapping the strength from her knees.

"Is that the sheriff's vehicle?"

"What else would Cliff drive?" The woman took hold of Ruby's arm to hurry her along.

"Why is he here?" Had the Las Vegas detective phoned the sheriff? Told him of the switch? If so, wouldn't he have alerted Ruby?

Beside her, the woman blew out an exasperated breath. "Because that's what men do when they're dating a woman. They show up unannounced and surprise her."

"Dating!" Ruby squeaked.

"Unless you have another definition for when a couple goes out six times in the past month."

Scarlett had a boyfriend. *Another* boyfriend besides Demitri. And he was the local sheriff!

A rush of anger steadied Ruby. Of all the details not to share, her sister had to pick the most important one.

CLIFF DEMPSEY SAT at the long oak table, a steaming mug of coffee in front of him. The next moment, he sprang to his feet and began pacing. What, precisely, was he doing here?

"Something wrong?" Sam asked.

His friend and owner of the Gold Nugget Ranch had joined Cliff in the empty kitchen. As recently as last week, a dozen guests would have competed for elbow room at the crowded table. Since completion of the new dining hall, the kitchen belonged solely to the staff.

"I probably shouldn't bother Scarlett when she's at work," Cliff said.

"Don't worry about it." Sam nodded at the bouquet of fresh flowers lying on the table. "You asking her to the square dance this weekend?"

"Yeah." Cliff nodded, wiping his damp palms on his khaki slacks.

As the law in these parts, he'd handled every situation from breaking up fights between drunken wranglers to singlehandedly taking down an armed bank robber to talking a possibly suicidal woman off the cell-phone tower at Grey Rock Point. Yet the prospect of inviting Scarlett McPhee to the dance had him sweating like a pig.

This was hardly their first date. It was, however, their first date after a recent lull. He and Scarlett had started out strong enough but this past week, she'd seemed to lose interest, not returning his calls and sounding distant when they did talk.

Cliff wasn't sure what to make of it. Could be something simple as her having a case of nerves. Just because he was considering taking their relationship from casual to serious and wanted to test the waters didn't mean she was, too. He was determined to find out.

"Nothing like waiting till the last minute." Sam dropped into an empty seat. "The dance is the day after tomorrow."

Cliff sat across from him. "I wasn't sure I could get the evening off." In truth, he'd stalled, doubting the wisdom of showing up unannounced. She may not appreciate it.

If he could go back in time to five minutes ago, he'd head straight to the station rather than call Sam's wife looking for Scarlett because, par for the course, she hadn't answered her cell phone.

"It's none of my business," Sam said, "but you want to tell me what's really bothering you?"

Cliff pushed his cowboy hat back on his head, then took it off and set it on the table. "My aunt Hilda thinks I should get married."

"It's a nice state to be in with the right woman. I can vouch for that."

"She thinks I should get married at the Mega Weekend of Weddings in June."

"Whoa!" Sam sat back. "Kind of soon, isn't it? That's only six weeks away. You and Scarlett haven't been dating very long."

"Real soon. Hilda has it in her head the local sheriff marrying will be a big draw. Bring more tourists to town for the event. Registration is only about half of what the town council hoped for."

Cliff's aunt not only owned the Paydirt Saloon, Sweetheart's most popular watering hole, she was also the mayor and a driving force behind the Mega Weekend of Weddings extravaganza.

The town of Sweetheart had a colorful history. It was founded by a pair of young lovers who met on a wagon train passing through. They married in California and returned to Sweetheart to settle down and raise a family. The man promptly discovered gold in the nearby mountains, and the town experienced its first boom.

Around the turn of the twentieth century, young couples began eloping to Sweetheart, their marriages officiated by a judge who didn't inquire too deeply into a person's age. The surrounding natural beauty drew tourists and outdoor recreationists, eager to hike, fish, horseback ride and, during the winter months, cross-country ski.

For the past fifty years, until the forest fire last summer nearly destroyed the town, the citizens of Sweetheart had capitalized on the wedding and tourist trade. Most of the local economy had depended on it for their livelihoods. When the tourists stopped coming after the fire, the economy died. Cliff's aunt, along with Sam and several dedicated others, was leading a fierce fight to restore Sweetheart to its former glory.

"She also thinks it will help with my reelection this fall," Cliff continued. "Hers, too. Not that anyone would run against her."

"You, either."

Sam had a point. A Dempsey had held the office of sheriff since the 1860s. It was a long-standing tradition the citizens were more than happy to continue.

"The mayor may be right, however." Sam sipped at his coffee. "You could be a draw. But is that any reason to get married? It's a huge step. Are you even in love with Scarlett?"

"No. But I like her. She's fun. Pretty. Smart. Good with kids."

"You sound like you're picking her out of a catalog. Might be why you're jumpier than a toad on a hot sidewalk."

Cliff had to laugh. "Rest assured, I'm not asking her to marry me or even considering it. My aunt will have to come up with another gimmick."

"Glad to hear that."

"But I'd like to see where things go with Scarlett. Test our potential."

Cliff had another, more personal reason for pursuing Scarlett he didn't share with his friend. He was a family man without a family of his own. A homebody without a full house to come home to. Last summer, he'd moved his newly divorced cousin Maeve back to Sweetheart and was now helping to raise her brood of three. His involvement with them served to emphasize how empty his personal life had become.

With the town's population of roughly one thousand, there weren't a lot of available women for Cliff to choose from. His job, the long hours and potential for danger, required an understanding wife, which narrowed the field even more. Scarlett McPhee, new to town, was a definite prospect.

Sam stood and clapped Cliff on the shoulder. "Take it from me, don't rush into anything. I married the first time for the wrong reasons, and we spent a lot of years making each other miserable."

At that moment, Sam's new wife Annie entered the kitchen. Cliff watched his friend's eyes light up and his smile grow wide. That never happened when Cliff looked at Scarlett. At least, not to the same degree.

It could, though. They might fall in love. Eventually.

Scarlett walked in behind Annie. Cliff ran a hand through his hair and did his best to flash her a smile as wide as his friend's. It froze, then waned. Judging by her wary expression, she wasn't at all happy to see him.

Damn. What was going on with her?

Annie greeted him with a warm, "Morning, Cliff," then winked at her husband. "Let's get out of here and leave these two alone."

Sam hesitated, his brows raised in question. Cliff shook his head. He didn't need backup. If he was going down in flames, he preferred to do it without an audience.

Once they were alone, he waited for Scarlett to speak. After a lengthy and awkward pause, he muttered, "Hey."

"Hi."

"Coffee?"

"Sure." Rubbing her palms together, she went to the counter and helped herself to a mug from the stack.

Cliff had been going to fix her the coffee. Instead, he watched, completely captivated. Scarlett glided across the room with an elegant—and subtly sensuous—grace he hadn't noticed before. As if she were wearing heels and not cowboy boots.

She took her coffee black. That was different. Maybe he and his cowboy tastes were rubbing off on her. The leather belt was also different. She usually didn't wear one. He found himself wishing she had. The belt accentuated her trim waist and ample curves, which were only hinted at before.

She raised the mug of coffee to her mouth, pursed her lips and blew on the liquid, then took a sip. A jolt Cliff hadn't felt in Scarlett's presence before arrowed through him. He'd always thought her to be attractive but not necessarily sexy. The sudden revelation unnerved him. He generally kept a firm grip on his emotions, a necessary skill in his line of work.

Picking up the bouquet, he said, "These are for you."

"Thanks." She accepted the flowers and, with both hands full, set them back down on the table. "You didn't have to."

"They're a bribe. I was hoping you'd go with me to the square dance Friday night."

The community center had finally reopened nearly a year after the fire. The barbeque and dance were in celebration.

"I…um…don't think I can. I appreciate the invitation, though."

"Are you going with someone else?" He didn't like the idea of that.

"No, no. I'm just…busy." She clutched her mug tightly between both hands.

"I'd really like to take you." Fifteen minutes ago, he probably wouldn't have put up a fight and accepted her loss of interest. Except he was suddenly more interested in her than before. These slight nuances in her were intriguing. "Think on it overnight."

"O…kay." She took another sip of her coffee. As she did, the cuff of her shirt sleeve pulled back.

He saw it then, a small tattoo on the inside of her left wrist resembling a shooting star. A second jolt coursed through him, this one of an entirely different nature. He hadn't seen the tattoo before.

Because, as of seven days ago when he and Scarlett ate dinner at the I Do Café, it wasn't there.

"Is that new?" He pointed to the tattoo.

Panic filled her eyes. "Um…yeah. It is."

Cliff didn't buy her story. There were no tattoo parlors in Sweetheart and, to his knowledge, she hadn't left town. And why the sudden panic?

Before he could question her further, his cell phone rang.

"Tom Welch just called," his deputy Iva Lynn said. "Seems some of his chain saws disappeared overnight from his garage. Though, knowing Tom, he probably lent it to a friend and can't remember."

"What's his address?"

"140 Matrimony Lane."

"Tell him I'll be there shortly." Cliff disconnected. "I'll call you later," he told Scarlett. And he would, if only to get to the bottom of her strange behavior and new tattoo that really didn't look all that new.

"All right."

Any other time, he would have given her a kiss. It felt strange under the current circumstances, so, instead, he opted for a brief, one-armed hug—which she tolerated more than returned.

The top of her head came to just under his nose. Cliff inhaled, only to pull back and stare at her.

Scarlett averted her face as if shy. Or she was hiding something. His police instincts told him it was the latter.

Leaning down, he took another whiff of the scent that had triggered his internal alarm. She smelled delightful, reminding him of the flowers he'd brought for her. It also wasn't at all how Scarlett normally smelled.

Something was seriously wrong.

He scrutinized her face. Eyes, chocolate brown and fathomless. Same as before. Hair, thick and glossy as mink's fur. Her lips, however, were different. More ripe, more lush and incredibly kissable.

He didn't stop to think and simply reacted. The next instant, his mouth covered hers.

She squirmed and squealed and wrestled him. Hot coffee splashed onto his chest and down his slacks. He let her go, but not because of any pain.

"Are you crazy?" she demanded, her breath coming fast.

Holding on to the wrist with the new tattoo, he narrowed his gaze. "Who the hell are you? And don't bother lying because I know you aren't Scarlett McPhee."

# Chapter Two

"Don't hurt me! Please."

Ruby had made the identical plea eight days earlier when she was accosted in her condo. The stalker hadn't listened and instead had increased his choke hold, starving her body of oxygen as he whispered vile things in her ears.

This man, Cliff, did listen. He released her but planted himself directly in her path, his stance and demeanor that of a linebacker. If she tried to run, she wouldn't make it three feet before he dropped her in her tracks.

"Who are you?" he repeated.

She wavered, forcing herself to concentrate as her heart banged against the side of her rib cage. He was the local sheriff. Sworn to serve and protect, yes? And Ruby, God help her, needed protection.

He was also someone her sister had liked well enough to date. Ruby should be able to trust him, only she didn't.

She cradled her wrist, the response more reflexive than anything else. He hadn't hurt her. Not really. But the kiss, and its suddenness, had startled her, releasing a flood of harrowing memories she'd give anything to forget.

"Are you okay?" he asked.

"No, I'm not." She'd never be okay again.

He reached for her wrist. "Let me see."

Alarmed, she retreated a step. He was already too close for comfort. "I'm fine."

"Tell me your name."

Ruby considered her answer. Lying, as he'd pointed out, was useless. He might arrest her. Probably would anyway. Either way, he'd find out very quickly she wasn't Scarlett.

"Ruby," she finally whispered. "Ruby McPhee."

"Scarlett's sister?"

She nodded. "Twin sister."

His eyes bore into her, noting, she supposed, the resemblances and very tiny differences that only their parents and close friends could distinguish. She averted her head and prepared herself for the onslaught of questions.

He asked only one. "Why?"

She instinctively knew her answer would decide his course of action. She settled on the truth, the lesser of two evils.

"I needed a place to hide out for a week or so." When he said nothing, she continued. "The detective on my case recommended it. At least until after the arraignment. So, Scarlett and I decided to trade places."

"Where is she?"

"San Diego. Visiting—" Ruby swallowed. Revealing that her sister was off reconciling with her old boyfriend probably wasn't a good idea. "A friend," she finished lamely.

"Who's arraignment? Yours?"

"Absolutely not!" He thought *she* was the criminal? Of all the nerve. "I was attacked last week. By a stalker. He was arrested and charged, then released on bail within hours." Ruby had barely left the station before an army of attorneys secured Crowley's freedom.

"Where did the attack take place?"

"My condo. He broke in and ambushed me when I came home."

"A former lover?"

There it was again, that accusatory tone. "No. We met at the casino where I work."

"A dealer?"

"I'm assistant manager of the VIP lounge. Crowley was a customer. Well, his father, actually. He's a regular and started bringing his son a few months ago after Crowley graduated college."

Ruby didn't tell Cliff more than that. She'd been advised to keep her mouth shut. The senior Crowley was a local politician with considerable clout. His lawyers had contacted Ruby twice, pressuring her to drop the charges in exchange for compensation.

It was yet one more reason she'd decided to leave Vegas until after Crowley's arraignment and why she would feel safer going home afterward. Once Crowley entered his plea, his attorneys would stop pressuring Ruby.

"Which casino?" Cliff asked.

How many questions was this guy going to ask? "The Century Casino. In Vegas."

"Did you encourage this guy? Why'd he pick you?"

Ruby frowned. Suddenly, their conversation had become an interrogation. She felt as if she was back at the police station, wanting to cry out that she was the victim, not the perpetrator.

"Contact Detective Dorell James of the Vegas Metro P.D. You can ask him the rest of your questions." She squared her shoulders. "Am I free to go now, Sheriff? Or are you taking me in?"

"I'm considering it."

An indignant gasp escaped her. "I haven't broken any laws."

"That remains to be seen. Your sister's missing."

"I told you. She's in San Diego. Call her if you don't believe me."

"I will. After I verify your story." Removing a satellite phone from his belt, he punched numbers into the keypad and offered no greeting to whoever answered. "I need you to locate a Detective Dorell James, LVMPD. Patch me through once he's on the line. Tell him it's regarding Ruby McPhee. Yes, that's right. Ruby. Not Scarlett."

He watched her while he waited, like a predator studying its prey in the seconds before pouncing. Ruby tried not to squirm and observed him in return through lowered lashes.

The sheriff—it was hard to think of him as Cliff—was one of those men who did justice to a uniform. Tall, broad shouldered, rugged features. She'd noticed his short cropped blond hair before he donned his hat and it disappeared beneath the brim. His eyes, pale blue when he looked into the light and gray when he looked away, were disarming. She doubted they missed the smallest detail, which must account for how he'd so easily discovered her ruse.

Under different circumstance, Ruby would find him attractive. She didn't blame her sister for dating the sheriff in Demitri's absence. He was certainly better boyfriend material than a nomadic marine biologist. Not that Ruby was in the market for a boyfriend.

She caught herself fidgeting and immediately stopped. The sheriff, for his part, hadn't so much as blinked.

This would be over soon, she told herself. Once Detective James explained her situation, surely the sheriff would release her…and probably go straight to the owner of the ranch.

She should have chosen a different town, gone to stay with her father in North Dakota. Not agreed to Scarlett's harebrained scheme. Too late now. She and Scarlett were both going to suffer the consequences—Scarlett losing her job and Ruby enduring a grueling visit to the station.

"Detective James. This is Sheriff Cliff Dempsey from Sweetheart, Nevada."

Ruby straightened.

"I have a woman here claiming to be Ruby McPhee. She's been impersonating her sister, Scarlett McPhee." After a pause, he handed the phone to Ruby. "He'd like to speak to you."

Ruby accepted the heavy phone, its weight and solid form oddly comforting. "Hello."

The detective's rich baritone filled her ears, also comforting. "Are you okay?"

How often had she been asked that question in recent weeks? Fifty? A hundred? Twice in the previous two minutes. "Yes."

"What happened? You only arrived in Sweetheart an hour ago."

She couldn't very well tell him that the sheriff had kissed her and instantly concluded she wasn't Scarlett. "I think my tattoo tipped him off."

"You're going to have to be more careful if you intend to pull this off."

"Yeah." It was a stupid mistake.

"Might be to your benefit if I fill him in."

Detective James didn't need to spell it out. Crowley had easily found the address of Ruby's condo. With his father's powerful connections and a full week at his disposal, he could possibly discover where she was hiding.

"Your call, Ruby."

"All right. Tell him." She handed the phone back to Sheriff Dempsey, looking away but listening raptly to his side of the conversation. Thankfully, it didn't last long. From what she gathered, reports and a photo of Crowley would be forwarded to the sheriff's office.

"I'll keep you posted." Cliff disconnected from Detective James and immediately placed a second call. "Your sister isn't answering," he said after a moment.

Ruby's head snapped around. "Why do you want to talk to her? Detective James confirmed my story."

"To verify that she's all right."

"She's fine."

Deep vertical creases formed between his brows. "Where is she?"

"I told you. San Diego."

"With a friend." He said the last word as if he knew darn well *boy* should be in front of it.

"Are you going to tell Sam and Annie about the switch?"

"Yes."

Worry seized her anew. "What if they fire Scarlett? She needs this job. And the fewer people who know about me, the better. I'm in danger. From the stalker *and* his family."

"Call your sister." His expression was all hard lines and uncompromising angles. "I want to speak to her."

Left with no other option, Ruby removed her cell phone from her shirt pocket and dialed.

"Put the call on speaker," Cliff said.

She did as told, refraining from rolling her eyes in exasperation. Scarlett answered on the fifth ring.

"Hi," Ruby's voice shook with relief.

"Sorry I didn't pick up sooner. Demitri was showing me the baby Beluga whale. It's so cute."

"Listen, we have a— "

"Oh, sis," Scarlett cut in. "Everything is just perfect. Demitri's being a dream." There was a wistfulness about her that even the speaker's tinny quality didn't distort. "He says he loves me and that he's sorry."

The sheriff's eyes darkened. He'd figured out Ruby wasn't her sister in a matter of minutes. He was surely connecting these dots at lightning speed. Was he hurt? Angry? Feeling betrayed? No one wanted to be the rebound.

Ruby dismissed an unbidden rush of guilt. Why did she care? She was hardly responsible for her sister's complicated love life.

The bouquet of flowers lying on the table caught her eye, and the guilt returned. The gesture was sweet. Thoughtful. That of a man who held affection for a woman.

If she hadn't asked for Scarlett's help, her sister might have stayed in Sweetheart.

Fat chance. The sheriff was history the second Demitri crooked his little finger. Ruby's appearance changed nothing.

"Scarlett," Cliff said into the phone. "Are you all right?" Each word was delivered with an icy undertone.

There was a long, awkward pause. Ruby half expected her sister to hang up. No matter. Cliff knew Scarlett was alive and well. That had been the whole purpose for the call in the first place.

Or, did he have an ulterior motive? He might have insisted Ruby call her sister in order to confirm the friend was indeed a *boy*friend. Maybe he was retaliating by embarrassing both Scarlett and Ruby.

Anger prompted her to blurt out, "He knows about us. He saw my tattoo."

The pause that followed was considerably shorter. "I'm sorry, Cliff," Scarlett said. "I didn't mean for you to find out this way. I'd have told you, but everything happened so fast."

"Are you all right?" he repeated.

"I'm great." She sighed. "Look, maybe we can talk about this when I have more time. Then, I can explain."

"Not necessary." Turning on his heels, he snatched his half-finished coffee off the table and carried it to the sink where he rinsed out the mug.

Ruby removed the phone from speaker before continuing the conversation with her sister.

"For crying out loud, Scarlett, why didn't you tell me about him?"

"I thought it was over."

"You thought?"

"All right, I wanted it to be over. When Demitri contacted me last week, I blew Cliff off. Sort of."

"Sort of? Really?"

"I avoided him. Didn't return his calls. I figured he'd get the message."

"He obviously didn't. He brought you flowers."

"Oh."

"You should have leveled with him." Ruby found it difficult to keep the disappointment from her voice. Her sister thought first of herself, then others.

"How's he doing?"

Now she suddenly cared?

"I have no idea." Ruby stared at Cliff's rigid back, then at the flowers on the table, and her heart cried a little for him.

"How are *you* doing?" Scarlett asked.

"Well enough, all things considered." She returned to the subject of Cliff. "Detective James says Sheriff Dempscy is someone I can trust. A straight-up guy."

"He is. And he's really sweet. If not for Demitri, I'd still be going out with him."

Second choice. Ruby decided to spare Cliff that tidbit of info.

"He's gorgeous, as I'm sure you've noticed," Scarlett continued, talking more to herself than to Ruby. "And I liked the attention. Demitri was being his typical indifferent self, and I needed a distraction."

Ruby gnashed her teeth together in frustration. How many times would her sister keep returning to that loser before she wised up?

The "gorgeous" guy in question stood at the sink, staring out the window, the muscles in his neck corded with tension.

Whatever Ruby did next, stay or leave, was partially up to him. She wasn't reassured. There was nothing yielding or compassionate about him as far as she could tell. Even his kiss had been hard. Void of emotion. She was nothing more to him than a lead in a possible crime.

And he was definitely not the person in whose hands she cared to place her fate.

A click alerted her there was a call waiting. "I have to go," she told Scarlett. "Someone's buzzing in."

"Sorry about Cliff."

"I'm not the one you should be apologizing to."

"Call me later."

"I will." Ruby checked the display, aware of Cliff's intense scrutiny. The incoming number wasn't one she recognized.

"Who is it?" he demanded.

"I'm not sure." Her new number was only a few days old.

Normally, she'd let the call go directly to voice mail. If it was important, they'd leave a message. But Cliff's intimidating presence threw her off balance.

She swiped her finger across the phone's screen, accepting the call. "Hello."

"Hey, baby. Miss me?"

Terror froze her bones. For a nanosecond. Then, fury took its place, just like it had that night in her condo. A fury that had ultimately saved her life.

"How did you get this number?" she rasped.

"You should know you can't hide from me forever. I'll always find you."

Her arm shook so violently, the phone started to slip. Using both hands, she held it in front of her mouth and screamed into the receiver, "Leave me alone!"

Cliff materialized at her side. Grabbing the phone from her, he barked, "Who is this?" Empty silence answered him, and the display returned to the home screen.

Crowley had hung up.

Ruby's legs went out from under her, and she leaned against the nearest solid object, which happened to be Cliff.

"Here, sit." Cliff lowered Ruby into a seat at the table, then fetched her a bottle of water from the fridge. He held it to her mouth. "Drink this."

She complied, and the water seemed to restore her strength. "The bastard," she muttered.

Cliff couldn't agree more.

She pressed her palms to her cheeks. "I don't understand. How did he find me? I changed my number three days ago."

"He may not have found you, only your new number. Let's assume for the moment you're still safe."

"I'm not assuming anything." Her hands fell, and she lifted her gaze to him. Tears shone in her eyes, making them large and luminous. "That's what got me in trouble in the first place. I assumed his creepy attention was a harmless crush. When he started cornering me at work and outside my condo building, I assumed complaining to my manager would resolve the problem. I also assumed I was safe inside my own home."

"Detective James said you fought him off."

"I never guessed for one second anyone could make it past the locks on my door or my security system."

"It's easier than you think."

"He came out of nowhere and grabbed me." Her hand drifted to her throat. "I couldn't breathe. Felt myself passing out. Then something snapped inside me. I got angry. How dare he intrude into my home! Violate me. I drove the heel of my stiletto into the top of his foot. Luckily, he was wearing shorts and sandals and my aim was good. He loosened his grip."

"You ran?"

"That would have been the smart thing to do." She chuckled mirthlessly. "Instead, I turned and kicked him square in the center of his man parts."

Cliff kept a straight face. Inside, he cringed, thinking of her pointed-toe shoe. Crowley deserved no less.

"He sank to his knees. That's when I ran into the hall as fast as I could. I went from door to door, screaming at the top of my lungs and ringing bells."

"You were brave to take him on."

"I was stupid. He could have killed me. I'm lucky he didn't."

"What did he do?"

"Got the hell out of there. By then, two or three of my neighbors had called 9-1-1. Another one of them took me inside her place to wait for the police. When Detective James arrived, I ID'd Crowley. They picked him up at his home a short while later. He denied attacking me, of course. But my neighbor saw his face when he pushed past her and was able to pick him out of a lineup. And then there was the injury to his foot."

Ruby shuddered.

Cliff put a hand on her shoulder. She'd been through a lot. He didn't tell her that this was only the beginning. A long road lay ahead of her. Opening the back of her phone, he removed the battery and SIM card.

"What are you doing?"

"Disabling your phone so he can't trace the signal. Don't reassemble it whatever you do." He set the phone on the table near her elbow.

She glared at the components as if they were Crowley himself. "I shouldn't be surprised he found my number. He learned everything else about me. My schedule at work. My friends. My route home."

"Is he connected?" In Cliff's experience, only someone with extensive resources or a computer hacker could find a newly issued cell-phone number.

"The mob? No. But his father's a congressman. The family is as rich as Midas."

Money. That explained a lot. Cliff was more anxious than ever to read the reports.

"Finish your water." He pushed the bottle toward her.

She'd stopped trembling but was white as a ghost. He

probably should have been easier on her. She didn't deserve to bear the brunt of his anger at her sister.

Anger or hurt?

Fine, he'd admit it. Scarlett dumping him for an old boyfriend had dented his ego. Which beat the heck out of broken heart, he supposed. If anything, Cliff had dodged a bullet. He should be grateful to the slob.

Removing his phone from his belt, he dialed the station.

"Who are you calling?"

"Detective James."

Ruby nodded resignedly. She sat finishing her water while Cliff was put through a second time to the LVMPD. Detective James expressed appropriate concern.

"Can you post a watch on her?" he asked.

"Consider it done."

At his remark, Ruby arched her brows.

Lovely brows, he observed. Elegant and graceful.

Cliff warned himself to stay strong. Women in trouble were a weakness of his and had landed him into trouble before.

"She needs to pull off this switch with her sister," Detective James said. "Crowley's one sly pervert, and he's not the kind to give up easily, as his previous record shows."

"I'll do everything I can."

Cliff finished his conversation with the detective, promising to check in with the man on a daily basis. For his part, Detective James would bring Crowley into the station for another face-to-face. There'd be repercussions for him violating the order of protection.

"Here's what we're going to do." Cliff took the seat next to Ruby. "Detective James agrees with me that while Crowley found your number, he has no idea you're in Sweetheart."

"You can't be sure."

"Which is why James is putting a tail on Crowley. In the

meantime, we're going to keep pretending you're Scarlett. It makes the best sense. He's after you, not her."

"Forget it. Obviously I'm no good at pretending to be Scarlett. I didn't fool you for even five minutes."

"I'll help you pull it off. On two conditions."

She sent him a look.

"First, you need a new cell phone. Better yet, I'll buy it for you. A disposable one. The only people you give the number to are your sister, Detective James, me and Sam."

"Scarlett's boss?"

"He and Annie need to be included."

"They'll fire Scarlett."

"They won't. Not after I talk to them."

Ruby pursed her mouth. Her pretty mouth.

Cliff had kissed it. Solely to discern her identity. If he were to do it again...

No. That kind of thinking had to stop this instant. Ruby McPhee was duty. Obligation. Nothing more.

"I'm not sure..."

"Sam's the kind of guy you want in your corner," Cliff said. "He'll understand why you and your sister switched places."

"I can't put the ranch in danger." Determination flashed in her eyes. The kind of determination that had caused her to act quickly during the attack. "Not the owners and certainly not their guests. I'll just stay in the trailer until the arraignment."

"Use your head, Ruby. This guy's looking for you and, by your own admission, he's smart and resourceful. He can track Scarlett to Sweetheart in hopes of finding you."

"My point exactly. The trailer's safe. I'll be out of sight."

"You'll be a sitting duck. The lock on that tin can wouldn't keep out a five year old."

"I'll install a new one."

"Which will hold him off for a minute at most."

He could see his argument was beginning to make sense to her. Also that, despite the brave front she put up, she was scared.

"I'll have a dead bolt installed. Just in case. And window locks. Leave the bedroom light on at night. Either me, my deputy or Sam will drive by every hour. If the light's off, we'll investigate."

"Sam? I can't ask that of him."

"Knowing Sam, he'll insist. And because a lot can happen in an hour, I'll post a guard."

"A guard?" Her eyes widened.

"The best one around. No one gets past him."

"Who is he?"

"You'll see. I'll bring him by tonight."

"I didn't intend to involve anybody else when I came here. This is my problem."

"We take care of our own in Sweetheart."

"But I'm not from Sweetheart."

"Your sister is. And you are by association."

She looked as if she didn't quite believe his reason. Well, Cliff didn't quite believe it, either. His interest in Ruby and his desire to help her went beyond civic responsibility.

"What's the second condition?" she asked.

"You go with me to the square dance tomorrow."

"You're kidding, of course."

"If you're going to pretend to be Scarlett, you have to lead her life. She and I are—were—seeing each other. Also, the more we're together, the more I can protect you. If Crowley finds his way to Sweetheart, he'll think twice about approaching you with me in the picture."

She dropped her head and groaned.

"I understand it's a lot to take in all at once."

"That's an understatement."

"You need to decide quickly, Ruby. We're already drawing attention by spending so much time in here alone."

"I suppose you're right. About telling Sam and Annie."

"They'll help you with the ins and outs of Scarlett's job."

"Her job!" Ruby's gaze darted to the clock on the wall. "I'm supposed to be leading a trail ride in thirty minutes." She shot to her feet. "I forgot all about it."

"Relax."

"Oh, God. I have no idea what I'm doing. This was an insane idea. One of the other wranglers will have to take over for me.

"Don't worry." Cliff steered her out of the kitchen. "They always send two wranglers."

At the front door, she dug in her heels. "I haven't been on a horse in eleven years. And I've never ridden in the mountains before."

He turned her toward him and gripped her by the shoulders. "You can do this."

"I don't think so."

"Sure you can. You fought off Crowley by yourself. Compared to that, a trail ride is a piece of cake." He made an instantaneous decision. "And I'll be with you the entire time."

# Chapter Three

Ruby struggled not to squirm beneath Sam Wyler's intense scrutiny.

"Man, it's weird." He knocked back the brim of his cowboy hat and scratched his forehead. "I can't tell you apart."

At least he hadn't kissed her in order to determine who was who.

"I'm sorry about trying to fool you," Ruby said.

"I understand why you did it. You're scared, and it sounds like you have good reason to be." He gave her another lingering once-over. "Scarlett mentioned a sister but not that you two were twins."

"If you don't want me filling in for her, it's quite all right." Despite Cliff's advice that she play the part of Scarlett, Ruby remained convinced hiding out in the trailer was the best option.

"I have no problem. As long as you can ride."

"It's been a while, but I think I can manage. Learning the trails may take a few days."

"I'm going with her," Cliff volunteered.

He hadn't left her side once from the moment they exited the house. They'd found Sam and a wrangler readying horses for the trail ride—something Ruby, or Scarlett, should be doing as part of her job. Sam must have stepped in to help when she and Cliff took so long in the kitchen.

Across from the corrals, guests milled about, watching

the process of saddling a dozen horses with either fascination, excitement or, in the case of one middle-aged woman,
stark fear.

"I'll go on the ride instead of her," Sam offered.

Cliff countered the suggestion. "I think she should stick
to Scarlett's regular job routine. She'll draw less attention
that way."

"What about the guests?" Ruby asked. "Will they be
safe?"

"Crowley doesn't like crowds. Even when he approached
your coworker, it was at night, in an empty parking lot."

That much was true. Detective James had explained to
Ruby that she was Crowley's target. He had no real interest
in anyone else, other than as a means to get to her.

"He especially won't do anything with me along," Cliff
added.

"Aren't you on duty?" She remembered him getting a call
back in the kitchen that had sounded official.

"I am. But I'll have my deputy cover for me."

Cliff's tone implied a twin impersonating her sister was
probably the highlight of his year. In a town of barely one
thousand mostly peaceful citizens, Ruby doubted much happened.

Sam turned to her. "Luis will lead the ride. You and Cliff
can bring up the rear, seeing as you're already attached at
the hip."

Ruby's cheeks warmed with embarrassment.

Cliff appeared unaffected.

She silently cursed his ability to remain cool, calm and
collected.

"Keep an eye peeled for Crowley or any suspicious
strangers while we're gone," Cliff warned Sam. He'd had
Ruby give Sam a rough description when they first talked.

"Are you really sure you're okay with this?" She couldn't

stop fretting about Sam and his family. "You have two young daughters. I'd hate putting you and them in danger."

"Cliff says the danger's minimal. For the moment."

"Yeah." It was that "for the moment" that concerned Ruby. She'd believed she was safe in her condo. Look how wrong she'd been.

"If for any reason the situation changes," Cliff addressed Sam, "you'll be the first person I tell. After Ruby."

She released a worried sigh.

"If Crowley and his resources track your sister here, all they'll report back to him is that Scarlett McPhee is alone and doing her job as usual. It should be enough to deter him."

"What about my car? It's parked beside the barn. Scarlett drives a Jeep."

"We need to move it out of sight right away."

"If you want," Sam said, "I'll park it in the barn while you're on the ride."

Ruby dug in her pocket and extracted her keys. How was she going to get around?

Sam must have read her mind. "Can you drive a stick?"

She nodded.

"We've got an old Chevy half-ton pickup you can use. Scarlett's driven it before on errands."

Ruby was touched by his generosity. "I can't impose on you more than I have."

He smiled kindly. "We're not going to let anything happen to you."

Her sister's boss was clearly a good man, if a little crazy for going along with the switch and all it entailed. "You owe me nothing," Ruby reminded him.

"Oh, don't think you're getting off scot-free. You'll have to work. Pretty hard, some days."

"I'm used to it." She hadn't risen to the position of assistant manager in two years by being a slacker.

Today might be different, however. She was running on pure adrenalin. When her lack of sleep and acute anxiety caught up with her, her energy level would plummet.

"Well then, let's see what you're capable of," Sam said. "Starting now."

Ruby glanced around. In the time they'd been talking, Luis had finished with the horses. All twelve stood shoulder to shoulder, tied to the fence.

"Which one's mine?" she asked, evaluating the selection from a distance.

"None of those." Sam started for the corral, motioning to Ruby when she was slow to follow. "Your sister's favorite is Mama Bear."

The remaining horses came over to greet the newcomers, seeking a petting. Good, solid, dependable stock, Ruby decided. Trustworthy enough for the most beginner of riders and capable of giving the experienced ones a run for their money.

Ruby took an instant liking to Mama Bear. With a prominent nose ridge, the medium-size dapple gray was no beauty. But her eyes were gentle and the hair on her muzzle was softer than peach fuzz.

Sam nodded approvingly. "She'll go all day long if you ask her."

Cliff settled on a handsome brown gelding that followed him to the gate like a puppy dog, then nearly ran him over in his haste to join his pals on the ride.

In the tack shed, Ruby perused the equipment. It was of good quality and sound condition. There were also helmets for those riders wanting extra protection. The Gold Nugget Ranch didn't take any risks when it came to their guests and employees.

Except for letting her ride along with them.

Ruby prayed Cliff and Detective James were right about Crowley and that the danger to others was minimal.

Locating Scarlett's bridle, saddle and blanket on the rack, she carried them to where Mama Bear was tied. It really was like riding a bike. The leather straps felt familiar in her hands, as did the smell and sound of horses. She'd missed being around them. Funny, the different paths her and Scarlett's lives had taken.

Cliff also knew his way around a horse and was ready to mount before her. He strode over. "Need a boost?"

"No, thanks."

She placed her foot in the stirrup and swung up into the saddle, not quite as nimbly as she'd hoped but still confident. She wriggled, trying to find a comfortable position. Unfortunately, it wasn't possible. Her stirrups were too long. Without adequate support, she'd slip and slide going up and down the mountains. Grabbing hold of the saddle horn, she moved to dismount.

"Stay."

At the abrupt order, she glanced down at Cliff.

"I'll get them," he said.

Before she could muster a protest, he took hold of her ankle and removed her foot from the stirrup. Next, he unfastened the buckle and raised the stirrup two notches.

"I can do that," she insisted.

"No problem." He finished and guided her foot back into the stirrup, his hand remaining on her heel.

She could feel the pressure of his strong fingers through the thick hide of her boots. It wasn't unpleasant. Then, his hand skimmed up her calf.

"How's that?" he asked.

"Nice…" Ruby caught herself. "I mean, good." She put weight in her heel, testing the stirrup's length.

He went around to her left side and repeated the process. For some reason, he seemed to take considerably longer than necessary.

Leaning down, she whispered, "Hurry. People are watching."

They were. The guests and Luis, all of them astride their various mounts, were waiting for the ride to start. Ruby was used to a certain amount of attention at work. This was different.

"Done." Cliff let the second stirrup drop. Then, with an agility Ruby wished she'd shown, he mounted the gelding.

Her resolve promptly deserted her. She'd always been attracted to men who could sit a horse well. Figured Cliff Dempsey, sheriff of Sweetheart and her sister's romantic castoff, would be one of them.

Fifteen minutes into the ride, the group abandoned the main road in favor of a well-used trail that was wide enough for two horses to walk abreast. Cliff kept pace with Ruby, his expression unreadable. For her part, she said nothing, unsure of what to say.

As the morning sun rose higher in a brilliant blue sky, many of the guests shed their sweaters and jackets, either tying them around their waists or behind their saddles. Ruby attempted to do her job by keeping an eye on the riders ahead of her and answering questions. The horse-related ones were simple enough. Cliff had to step in and assist with those concerning the region.

Eventually, the group settled down as the newness of the ride wore off and they became more comfortable with their mounts. Ruby's mind drifted, lulled by the rhythmic clip-clopping of hooves on the hard ground and sunlight flickering over her face as it filtered through the sprawling tree limbs.

This day, this entire situation was surreal. Unbelievable. Yesterday, a mere twenty-four hours earlier, she'd been getting dressed for work. Then, her manager called to say that Crowley had showed up at the casino *again* and was asking about her. When the manager insisted Crowley leave, he became physical and shoved the manager aside. Ruby, in turn, contacted Detective James.

After that, everything went crazy. By evening, she and Scarlett were on the phone, putting together the finishing touches on their plan.

And now she was here. Riding a horse for the first time in eleven years and leading—correction, following—a trail ride. She was also attending a square dance on Friday night with the local sheriff. Whom she'd kissed.

Surreal didn't begin to describe it. *Un*real was more like it.

"This is my first time on a horse."

A child's voice penetrated the thick layer of Ruby's thoughts. She blinked herself back to the present.

While she'd been wool gathering, a young girl on a compact horse had fallen behind the others and was riding beside Ruby. Cliff, she discovered after a quick glance around, was now behind her.

"It is?" Ruby felt compelled to respond.

"I like riding." The girl grinned, showing front teeth too big for her face.

Ruby had no clue as to her age. She knew next to nothing about kids. Not that she didn't like them. She and her circle of friends weren't yet mothers, and she had little exposure to anyone under the age of twenty-one in her line of work. Ruby wasn't bothered by her lack of skills. She'd long ago decided she was born minus the mothering gene.

Another difference between her and her sister. Scarlett adored kids and intended to produce a passel of her own one of these years.

"That's nice," Ruby muttered, glancing around. Where were the girl's parents? Shouldn't they be supervising her?

"I want to be a cowgirl when I grow up," the girl continued. "Like you."

"It's hard work. Long days. You won't have much time

for anything else. Forget having a boyfriend. Forget any kind of social life."

Ruby was remembering her youth. She'd been determined to compete nationally in Western pleasure classes and succeeded three years running. She'd sacrificed a lot to get there, including things most teenagers took for granted.

Unfortunately, in all her attempts, she'd failed to place higher than twelfth. Disappointment soured her. It was the reason she'd quit riding altogether after high school and moved to Vegas. No more chasing pipe dreams, she'd told herself.

Until today, she hadn't realized how much she missed riding. Her father was fond of saying that horses were good for the soul. Relaxing into the sway of the saddle and gazing at the distant mountains, she could almost forget her troubles.

Almost. Cliff's eyes boring into her back were a constant reminder of her present circumstances.

"I'm a hard worker," the girl piped up.

"I'm sure you are."

"My mommy bought me this." She released the reins long enough to pat the top of her neon-pink cowboy hat.

"It's bright."

"And these." She stuck out her foot to show off a matching pink boot.

"Mmm." Ruby mustered a smile that, judging from the girl's pout, was sorely inadequate.

What did she want? For Ruby to enthuse endlessly about her recent purchases?

"Every cowgirl needs a good hat and a sturdy pair of boots," Cliff said. "Especially pink ones."

At his comment, Ruby turned in the saddle to stare. Had he really just said that?

The girl also turned, beaming from ear to ear. "I still need a vest. With fringe."

"Don't forget spurs."

Her eyes widened. "Can girls wear those?"

"Sure they can. And you'll need a rope, too."

"Wow!" She pulled back on her reins, slowing her horse until she was riding alongside Cliff.

Ruby clucked to Mama Bear, feeling officially dumped. So much for being a female wrangler and the girl's idol.

"Can you teach me to rope?" the girl asked Cliff.

"I don't work for the ranch, but I'll show you a few pointers when we get back from the ride."

"Cool. Mommy!" she shouted over Ruby's head. "The man is going to teach me to rope."

A woman three horses up glanced over her shoulder, mild concern on her face.

"You're welcome to join us, ma'am." Cliff tipped his hat. "And the rest of your family."

The woman's features relaxed. "All right, I guess."

Figured Cliff would be good with children. From what Ruby could tell, he was close to perfect. Her sister really would have been better off picking him over Demitri.

Someday, eventually, Ruby would date again. Maybe when Crowley was safely behind bars. Until then, even the close-to-perfect Sheriff Dempsey would remain strictly eye candy.

"Did you barrel race, too?"

It took her a second to realize Cliff had addressed her and not the young girl. They were once more riding side by side, and the girl was with her mother. When had that happened?

Ruby really needed to concentrate.

"No, only Scarlett. I competed in Western pleasure. The closest I got to rodeoing was team penning, which I did only because I thought it was good training for my horses. Sharpened their skills. Mine, too."

"But doesn't your dad train barrel racers?"

"He does. And my mom breeds and raises them." Ruby didn't correct herself. She still talked about her parents as if they were married to each other and not to different people. The habit was a hard one to break.

"So how did you get into showing horses?" Cliff asked.

"I know, it's strange, me coming from a rodeo family."

Even more strange was her talking so causally with Cliff about her past. As if he wasn't here solely for the purpose of protecting her from a dangerous stalker.

"I like team penning," he said. "Maybe we can try it one day."

"As partners or competitors?"

"Either one."

Was that a glint of amusement in his eyes? She must be mistaken.

"What about you? Where did you learn to ride?" Only after she voiced the question did she realize she was truly interested.

"I grew up in Sweetheart. We're a ranching community."

"I thought the town catered to the wedding trade."

"We did. Until the fire last summer destroyed the local economy."

"Scarlett said things were getting better."

"They are. Slowly. We went from hosting fifty weddings a month to zero. We're up to about five now. The town council is hoping to change that with the Mega Weekend of Weddings."

It was a shame the tourists had stopped coming, Ruby thought. The charming community was situated amid some of the Sierra Nevada's most spectacular scenery.

Formerly spectacular scenery, she reminded herself. While the area surrounding the Gold Nugget Ranch had been untouched, a large part of the region was laid to waste by the fire's ferocious appetite.

"Ranching is our second largest industry," Cliff said. "Prospecting, cross-country skiing and hiking all run a close third."

"You're from a ranching family?"

"No, but I worked at the Triple C Ranch from the time I was fourteen until I left for police academy. In between helping my aunt out at the Paydirt."

Something Ruby's sister said last night about the popular saloon rang a bell with her. "Your aunt's the mayor."

"Twelfth one from the Dempsey family. And I'm the eighth sheriff."

Ruby drew back. "You're not kidding."

"A family tradition. We have a lot of them here. My uncle owns the general store. Sam's wife's family owned and operated the Sweetheart Inn for fifty years. It burned down in the fire so now Annie and her mother help Sam run the Gold Nugget as well as oversee the Sweetheart Memorial. The Yeungs' ancestors settled here during the 1870s when the railroad came through. As did a lot of other families."

Sweetheart wasn't just a small town. Its citizens were a large extended family.

How had her wanderlust-loving sister wound up here?

Demitri's last breakup, Ruby answered herself. Scarlett had been heartsick, as usual, quit her job and found a new one here. Miles away from San Diego.

Sadly, her sister would likely follow the same path again. Cliff was lucky he got out when he did. Before he fell head over heels for Scarlett.

Ruby recalled the bouquet of flowers. Had he fallen already?

Did she care one way or the other?

"You're a natural," she observed, inclining her head in the direction of the young girl.

"I'm used to young kids. My cousin has three. Two girls and a boy. Seven, five and two respectively. She's a single working mom, so I help out when I can."

"You babysit your nieces and nephew?"

"The term's subjective. My cousin claims I'm merely an adult presence in the room."

Ruby suspected he was wonderful with them and that they adored him.

How was it some woman hadn't snatched him up yet? From all accounts, he was a catch.

"Look, there's the ranch," someone called out.

They'd reached the top of a gently sloping hill. In the distance, about a mile away by Ruby's estimation, was the ranch, the main house and outbuildings, recognizable by their distinctive shapes. The ride was nearing its end.

To her surprise, Ruby felt a stab of disappointment and not just because she'd enjoyed being on horseback. Cliff's company was a welcome diversion from the constant worry and stress she'd been dealing with since Crowley had first come into the casino and chosen to target her simply because she'd discouraged his inappropriate attention.

Then again, she reminded herself, Cliff wouldn't be far away for very long. There was the square dance Friday night and his regularly checking in with her.

The prospect reassured her. Cliff was capable and committed to her safekeeping. It also sent a mild thrill coursing through her.

Great. Only a few hours into their acquaintance and she was already anticipating his company. What would she be like at the end of a week?

# Chapter Four

Cliff didn't let Ruby out of his sight. He watched her every move as she helped Luis with the guests. Most needed a hand dismounting, their legs wobbly after the hour-and-a-half ride. Many wanted to chat, their spirits raised by the fresh air, majestic scenery and small taste of cowboy life.

Because there would be a second trail ride later that morning, the entire string of horses was left saddled and bridled. Ruby and Luis tethered them to the corral fence. After warning their neighbors with a nip or squeal for getting too close, all the horses settled in for a well-deserved snooze.

The sight of them resting, their tails lazily swishing, reminded Cliff of the years he'd worked at the Triple C Ranch. Attending college and, eventually, police academy, had been a difficult decision. Cliff loved ranching that much.

But the Dempseys were the law in Sweetheart and had been since the days when the local sheriff wore a Colt .45 strapped to his side. Cliff had a tradition to carry on and didn't regret leaving the Reno P.D. in order to return to Sweetheart. He'd taken to the job of sheriff just like his father and the multitude of grandfathers and great uncles before him.

What he did regret was his one stupid blunder—becoming involved with a witness. It hadn't cost him his career; the reprimand had been light. But it did blow a case a year in the making and it left a mark on his otherwise untarnished record.

It had also cost him the complete trust of his commanding officer and partner and cut his chances for advancement in half.

"You said you'd teach me to rope."

Cliff glanced down at the cowgirl in pink and smiled. "That I did."

"My brother wants to learn, too." She presented a reluctant young cowboy, a good foot shorter than she.

Cliff wasn't sure about the boy wanting to rope. He appeared more inclined to watch and suck his thumb than participate.

"You don't mind?" The children's mother had come up behind them. She also wore newly purchased boots from the looks of them. Brown, not pink.

"My pleasure. But I don't have much time." He had rounds to make before returning to the station, and the pile of paperwork on his desk never seemed to shrink. He was also anxious to read the reports on Crowley that Detective James was sending over.

"If you're too busy…"

"Quite all right, ma'am." He winked at the girl. "I made this young lady a promise. Wait right here."

With one eye on Ruby, he strode toward the tack shed. She was engaged in conversation with Will Dessaro, the ranch's trail boss and Scarlett's immediate supervisor. Judging by Will's unconcerned features, he believed he was talking to Scarlett. Ruby appeared to be handling herself, although she'd shoved her hands into her jeans pockets. A sure sign she was on edge.

Cliff hated the idea of leaving her to fend for herself, but he had no choice. Sam had promised to watch her in Cliff's absence. She wouldn't be going on the next trail ride. Instead, Sam had assigned Ruby some of the endless chores around the barn and corrals.

Inside the tack shed, Cliff searched for a lariat. He found three hanging on the wall and picked the one best suited for a child. Even then, it was way too big.

The girl didn't care and grasped the rope with glee when he showed it to her.

"Come on." He led the mother and children away from the horses to the opposite side of the corral. An old tree stump provided the perfect practice target and a tall ponderosa pine offered ample shade. "We'll start with the basics. Watch me first, then you can try."

The girl was reluctant to surrender the lariat, but she did. Cliff adjusted the loop until it was the right size for him, then raised the lariat over his head and swung it in the air. At the right moment, he flicked his wrist and let the lariat fly. The loop landed around the tree stump with a satisfactory thwap, and he jerked the rope tight.

The little girl's mouth fell open, and she turned wide eyes on her mother. "Did you see that?"

"Very impressive."

"Do it again." The little boy spoke for the first time.

"Yes, yes," his sister insisted.

"Don't you want to try?" Cliff asked.

She shook her head so hard, her pink cowboy hat tilted sideways.

Wasn't that just like a kid? Cliff chuckled to himself. His own nieces were no different. Gung ho one second, timid as a mouse the next.

"What about you, partner?" The boy had once again ducked behind his mother's leg. "Ma'am? Would you like to give it a shot?"

She broke into a laugh. "Why don't I just take pictures? Do you mind?"

"Not at all." He threw the lariat again.

After some more coaxing, he finally convinced the girl to try her hand. Mom snapped more photos, enough to fill an album. The family left happy, the children dashing ahead of their mother as they climbed the tree-lined path toward the guest cabins.

"If that's how you are with kids, I'd say you're a whole lot better than an adult presence in the room."

Cliff spun at the sound of Ruby behind him. He hadn't noticed the differences in her and her sister's voices before. Ruby's was slightly deeper and a little huskier. Very sexy.

He had to stop comparing the two of them. He also had to stop thinking of her other than professionally. Cliff had crossed the line before. He would not make the same mistake twice.

"I'm the fun uncle," he said. "I let them get away with murder. If there's a rule, we break it. Makes my cousin mad."

"She's lucky to have you."

"I'm lucky to have her, too."

He and his cousin weren't just related, they'd grown up together and were good friends. More like siblings. Cliff had never cared much for her ex and wasn't sorry to see them divorced. Though, he was sorry for the pain his cousin and her children had endured.

"I'm not very good with kids," Ruby admitted.

Cliff had observed her awkwardness with the young girl during the ride. "There's no secret. Just show an interest in them."

"Scarlett loves kids."

"You shouldn't mention her name out in the open," he warned Ruby in a low voice.

"Sorry," she murmured and glanced about. "I don't think anyone heard."

"Walk with me."

"I can't just leave the guests."

Cliff reached for her hand and held up their laced fingers. "Hey, Will. I'm borrowing Scarlett for a few minutes. She'll be right back."

The trail boss gave them a wave. "Sure thing."

When Ruby would have removed her hand from Cliff's, he tightened his grip.

"Remember, we're dating. People expect to see us together."

"Are you going to kiss me again before you leave?"

He wasn't sure if she'd asked the question in jest or seriousness. "We'll compromise with a hug."

Her relief was visible. She'd been serious.

"Call me every hour on the hour," he told her when they reached his vehicle. "If you're more than five minutes late, I'll call you."

"My phone's in pieces, remember?"

"Use Sam's or Annie's or the ranch phone." He pulled a business card from his pocket, scribbled his cell number on the back and pressed it into her palm. "Don't lose this until you've memorized the number. Park the truck Sam lends you as close to the trailer as possible. And leave the porch light on all night."

"Porch light. Living room light. I'd better check my supply of bulbs. At this rate, I'll be going through them quickly."

She was putting up less of a fight than she had before the trail ride. Crowley's phone call was probably responsible.

"Good idea," he said. "Light is one of the best deterrents. Call me when you're ready to leave work. I'll meet you here and follow you home."

"With my guard?"

She'd remembered.

He smiled. "You'll like Sarge. Best partner I've ever had." As soon as he spoke the words, his smile faltered. Her sister hadn't like Sarge one bit. Maybe Ruby would have the same reaction.

"Sarge? Is he former army?"

"Retired from the police force. There isn't anyone else I trust more to protect you when I'm not around."

"Do I invite him in or does he sit outside in his vehicle?"

"Your choice. He'll be fine on the front porch."

"All night?"

"He's done it before."

"Maybe he can sleep on the couch," she said with great reluctance.

"Or in the kitchen." Cliff popped the automatic lock with his key fob and opened the driver's side door. "Remember to call me."

"Thank you for everything. Scarlett and I...we acted hastily. Without thinking things through."

"That happens when you're scared."

"Everyone's going to so much trouble for me."

"We'll talk more tonight. Set up your new cell phone. Make plans for the square dance."

"Okay." She started to back away.

Cliff didn't let her get very far before pulling her into his embrace.

"For show," he said. "In case Will and any of the other employees are watching."

And to comfort Ruby, he added to himself. She looked ready to crumble.

Only it felt less like show and comforting and more like how a man holds a woman he wants to kiss. Cliff was reluctant to release her.

"See you later." Sliding behind the steering wheel, he started the engine. She turned and headed back to the corral. He watched her progress in his rearview mirror.

Leaving Ruby was difficult and not only because he was concerned for her safety.

He couldn't remember the last time a woman had felt so good, so right, in his arms.

Cliff spent a total of fifteen minutes at Tom Welch's place

checking on the missing chain saw. While there were fresh footprints behind his barn, nothing was stolen or disturbed. Cliff considered the possibility that Tom had made the prints himself. He did have a reputation for imbibing one too many whiskeys, forgetting where he'd been and what he'd done.

After assuring Tom that either he or his deputy would drive by later on rounds, Cliff aimed his SUV in the direction of town. Traffic was light, and he passed only two unfamiliar vehicles. The occupants appeared to be tourists. Nonetheless, he made a mental note of each car's make and model.

The Dempsey Trading Post and General Store had changed little since Cliff was a kid, though it was easily ten times the size of the original one founded in the early 1860s. His ancestors had originally come from Ohio, traveling with one of many wagon trains heading west. For reasons unknown, they disembarked early rather than continuing to California.

Sweetheart was no more than a primitive settlement in those days. Cliff's entrepreneurial great-great-whatever uncle founded a one-room trading post that had catered to prospectors lured to the area by a gold strike in the nearby mountains. As the population expanded, so had the man's business. His nephew became the first sheriff.

Cliff grew up spending much of his youth in the store, pestering his aunt or playing with his cousin. Even during high school, when girls and sports consumed his every waking thought, he still visited the store. More frequently when his aunt hired the homecoming queen for a part-time cashier position.

Striding down the center aisle, he tipped his hat to a pair of customers and made his way straight to the photo and electronics counter.

"Hey, you!" His cousin Maeve smiled broadly at him as she rang up a young man's order. "Be just a second."

He observed his cousin, taking pleasure in her happy expression and relaxed, cheerful manner. So different from last summer when he'd helped her and her children move here. Then, she'd been miserable and withdrawn.

"What brings you by, cowboy?" she asked after seeing off the customer. "Don't tell me Evan is throwing rocks into the neighbor's yard again."

Lately, her two-year-old son had decided it was fun to collect rocks and chuck them over the fence. The neighbor had complained.

"Not that I've heard," Cliff said.

"Thank goodness." Maeve wiped imaginary sweat from her brow.

"I need to buy one of those disposable phones." He indicated the display wall behind her.

"Something happen to yours?"

"Nope."

She waited and shrugged when he didn't offer any additional information. "I'm guessing it's one of those sheriff things you can't tell me about."

"And you'd be right."

She showed him the three brands of phones the store carried and recommended the most popular one. He chose the least popular. If Crowley was going to get this number, he'd have to work extra hard.

"Need help activating it?"

"No, thanks." Cliff quelled her insatiable curiosity with a look.

She grumbled in frustration. "You really aren't going to tell me, are you?"

"Sorry."

"Will I see you at supper?" She bagged the box containing the phone. "Mom wants to talk about the Mega Weekend of Weddings." She rolled her eyes. "What else is new?"

"Can't. I'm on duty."

"You're allowed to take a meal break."

She was right. And he often did join his aunt and cousin for lunch or supper and sometimes breakfast if it was a tough night.

"I have other plans."

"More sheriff stuff?"

"What can I say?"

She made a last attempt to sway him. "The kids will miss you."

"I'll see them tomorrow." Cliff had volunteered to watch Maeve's lively brood in the evening while she helped her mother decorate the community center for the upcoming square dance.

Maybe Ruby would go with him to babysit. Scarlett had.

He reconsidered almost immediately, and it had nothing to do with Ruby's discomfort around children. She was a crime victim and, therefore, off-limits. They could carry out her ruse without spending every evening together.

"All right." Maeve sighed expressively. "If you change your mind, just call. Mom always makes enough food for an army."

Grabbing the bag with the phone, he bid his cousin good-bye and left the store. With no other calls coming in, he went directly to the station.

Only one other car occupied the small lot outside the station. It belonged to Iva Lynn, his dispatcher, secretary and, when the need arose, his deputy. She'd even filled in as sheriff for two months, in between the time Cliff's father retired and Cliff transferred from the Reno police force.

His parents had left behind a lifetime in Sweetheart to reside in Phoenix where the dry air and milder weather was kinder to his mother's arthritic joints. At first, Cliff wasn't thrilled about returning to the home of his youth. A big-city police force offered more opportunity. But then, there had been the incident with Talia.

His fault. No one else's. The only way he'd be able to

salvage his career and his pride was to start over. He didn't like thinking of himself as having returned to Sweetheart with his tail between his legs, but it felt like that some days.

Naturally, the townsfolk had welcomed him with open arms. The incident at the Reno P.D. was never mentioned.

Cliff wiped the dust from his boots on the mat outside the door, and then entered the large room that served as the sheriff's office. Right next door was the mayor's office.

Both rooms had been built onto the side of the community center. Across the lot was a metal building, which housed the town's fire engine and served as a base for the volunteer fire department. Adjacent to that was a helicopter landing pad for use in air-transport emergencies.

Luckily, this cluster of buildings was spared when the forest fire raged through town. The same couldn't be said for half of Sweetheart's homes and businesses. The town's recovery was painfully slow. Cliff's aunt was committed to accelerating the process. Her latest efforts included the Mega Weekend of Weddings.

A buzzer sounded as he opened the door. Iva Lynn didn't look up from her computer. "How's things at the Gold Nugget?"

"Morning. And they're fine."

What Iva Lynn really wanted to know was how the square dance invitation had gone with Scarlett. Like Cliff's aunt and cousin, Iva Lynn took too much interest in Cliff's personal life. Also like his relatives, she believed she had a right.

Iva Lynn had worked for Cliff's father during his entire career and, at the very start of her career, for Cliff's grandfather. The running joke in town was that Iva Lynn came with the position of sheriff. She might have reached the age of retirement, but she was far from retiring. Cliff wasn't the only one convinced the entire tiny department would fall to pieces without her.

Sarge roused from his resting place on the floor next to Cliff's desk and hop-walked over to him.

"Hey, buddy." Cliff bent and stroked the three-legged shepherd behind the ears. "How's it going?"

Sarge licked his hand in response.

"I have a job for you."

"What's that?" It was Iva Lynn who asked the question.

"I'm taking him over to Scarlett's trailer. He's staying there for a while."

"Why's that?" This time, Iva Lynn did glance up from her computer. "I thought she didn't like dogs."

While Sarge technically belonged to Cliff, Iva Lynn watched the dog during her days at the station. As such, she felt entitled to comment on his care, much like she felt entitled to comment on Cliff's personal life.

"*She* doesn't like dogs." Cliff had every intention of filling in Iva Lynn regarding the twins' switch. For one, he'd need her help making the hourly rounds. Also, she'd surely read the reports from Detective James as she printed them off.

"Who's Ruby McPhee?" Iva Lynn asked as if on cue. "Scarlett's sister?"

"Yes."

"She staying with Scarlett?"

"In a manner of speaking."

"Until her stalker is arraigned?"

"Give me a chance to read the reports. Then we'll talk." Cliff patted Sarge one last time and went to his desk, dropping the bag with the disposable phone on the corner before sitting. The dog hobbled back to his spot.

Sarge might be missing a hind limb, but Cliff had meant every word he'd told Ruby about his trust in the dog's ability to protect her. When danger was present, Sarge became a beast.

"Whatcha got there?" Iva Lynn stared pointedly at the bag.

"Don't you have schedules to complete?"

"They've waited till now. They can wait another two minutes."

Cliff was surrounded by curious women. This one stared him down until he answered her. "A cell phone."

"For who? You?"

"No."

"This Ruby McPhee?" Iva Lynn's carefully penciled brows bobbed like those of a ventriloquist's puppet. She was no dummy and might even now be putting two and two together.

Cliff ignored her and removed the reports on Crowley from his in-box. The stack was heavy. Also neatly ordered. Iva Lynn had definitely read the reports. He didn't ask her about the contents, wanting to process the information with a fresh eye.

"Any coffee left?" He glanced at the pot on the counter.

"You asking me to get it for you?" Iva Lynn's brows danced again.

"Wouldn't dream of it." He stood and helped himself to the remaining cup. Wincing at the strong taste, he added a second spoonful of sugar.

"We're low on filters, should you be near a store anytime soon."

"I'll pick some up later."

The bickering was all in fun. Deep down, the two were good friends and worked well together.

Cliff sipped his coffee as he leafed through the reports. Crowley's bio read like a case study straight out of a college psychology textbook. His mug shot raised the hair on Cliff's arms. It showed a normal-enough-looking young man, except for the demented gleam in his eyes.

Rumors had circulated about Crowley's father for years. A local congressman who'd used his wife's family name and bank account to win elections. More than powerful, he was power *hungry,* narcissistic and domineering. His string of mistresses was legendary. It included the likes of Playboy models, minor celebrities, other politician's wives and the most renowned madam in Vegas.

His wife, Crowley's mother, had emotionally checked out years ago. Her penchant for drugs, alcohol and younger men regularly made the tabloid headlines, along with pictures of her husband's latest marital infidelity. Crowley's picture, too, since the attack on Ruby.

His older brother was a clone of their father. In copies of reports from the elite boarding school the brothers had attended as teenagers, there were repeated mentions of bullying. More than once, Crowley had been found beaten. Though he would never admit to who'd inflicted his injuries, the school administration strongly suspected his older brother. With a history like that, it was no wonder Crowley turned out the way he had.

Ruby wasn't his first stalking victim by any means. There had been previous charges against him, brought by fellow students at the University of Nevada. The charges, however, were suddenly and inexplicably dropped.

Cliff suspected the victims were paid off, much as the family's attorneys were pressuring Ruby. He studied the photos of Crowley's other victims, observing the physical similarities to Ruby. The creep clearly exhibited a preference for pretty brunettes.

Cliff was no expert but what he saw in Crowley was the product of a severely dysfunctional family. Neglected at home, he sought love and acceptance elsewhere. When the women he targeted didn't appreciate his over-the-top-attention, he responded the way he'd been taught by his father and older brother. He forced himself on the women.

Slowly Cliff leafed through the remaining reports, stopping to read the police interview with Ruby. He was particularly interested in the history of her and Crowley's relationship.

She'd met him at work. His father had been a regular at the VIP lounge for years but only recently started bringing his twenty-two-year-old son with him. Though seven years separated Crowley and Ruby, he'd taken an instant liking to her and begun visiting the VIP lounge on his own. When he wasn't seated in her section, he'd ask to be moved, becoming insistent if he was refused and once making a scene.

Ruby had been nice to him, in the way she was nice to all patrons. Mild, harmless flirting was part of the job. Crowley, starved for attention and completely infatuated, mistook her niceness as affection. He started bringing her gifts, which she refused, citing policy. Then, he began approaching her outside the lounge when her shift was over.

Ruby had complained to her manager, and Crowley was asked, politely, to leave her alone. After that, he started following her home and confronting her at the entrance to her condo building or in the parking garage.

When asked why she didn't file a police report at the time, Ruby stated that Crowley really hadn't done anything other than make her feel uncomfortable. Her manager had promised to speak to Crowley's father. She also felt safe inside her condo.

Famous last words, Cliff mused. How many victims had assumed they were safe behind a locked door? How many thought their stalker would take no for an answer?

Ruby had been wise to get out of Vegas when she did. Crowley's stalking tactics had progressed in the past year, as his calculated attack on Ruby and the lengths to which he'd gone to track her new number proved. An arrest and possible pending trial were not scaring him off, either.

At the sound of his cell phone ringing, Cliff's hand jerked. It was Ruby, making her first hourly check in.

"Sheriff Dempsey."

"It's Ruby," she said in a low voice. "Calling as ordered."

He set the reports down, enormously glad to hear from her.

Detective James was right, this Crowley was one scary creep. Ruby would be in real danger if he ever found her.

## Chapter Five

Ruby shifted into second gear. The old truck accelerated slowly, groaning as it chugged down the hill. At the bottom, she turned onto the main road. A glance in her rearview mirror confirmed Cliff was behind her.

As promised, he'd arrived at the ranch to escort her home after work. She'd waited for him in the truck, not wanting to give him a chance to get close. The hug this morning had been awkward enough.

If she didn't know better, she'd think Sheriff Dempsey had enjoyed holding her. She'd enjoyed holding him—which was why she'd decided to nix any close contact.

Forcing herself to relax, she checked the rearview mirror again. This Sarge, whoever he was, must be meeting them at the trailer. As far as she could tell, Cliff was riding solo in his SUV.

The trip through town went slower in the truck than it had in her zippy compact car. Ruby was able to really take in the sights, something she hadn't done earlier.

Sweetheart was exactly as her sister had described it. Quaint, charming and picturesque. While not fully restored after the forest fire, easily half the homes and commercial buildings had been rebuilt or replaced. Everywhere she looked, redbrick chimneys climbed the sides of log houses, welcome signs decorated front doors and wildflowers bloomed in yards or along the road.

The town teamed with activity. She wasn't surprised to see cowboys on horseback, along with hikers, amateur prospectors and dirt-bike enthusiasts.

There were also couples of varying ages, holding hands or linking arms as they strolled the sidewalks. Little by little, Sweetheart was reclaiming its title as a popular tourist spot for exchanging vows. Ruby understood why. If she were to ever elope, this would be her destination of choice.

About a quarter mile from the trailer, Cliff suddenly pulled into the adjoining lane and passed her. By the time she reached the trailer, he was already parked and on foot. He met her at the truck, and she noticed he was wearing his gun. A shiver ran through her as she rolled down the window.

"Give me the key," he instructed in a no-nonsense tone. "Stay put until I give you the all clear."

"Do you really think Crowley's in there?" At Cliff's pointed stare and outstretched hand, she promptly did as told.

It was becoming a habit, this relinquishing of keys. First Sam and now Cliff. Ruby was feeling increasingly uncomfortable about the loss of control in her life.

Cliff entered the trailer slowly, calling out, "Sheriff's Department."

Had he pulled his gun? Ruby suppressed another shiver. So much for assuming she'd be safe in Sweetheart. It was no different than Vegas.

After a few minutes, he emerged and signaled to her with a wave. As usual, his expression was inscrutable.

"No Crowley?" she asked, meeting him on the porch.

"If you're thinking I'm going overboard—"

"I'm not. Just wondering if we'll be going through this same routine every day."

"Not with Sarge on duty."

"Speaking of which—" she glanced around "—I guess he's late."

"He's in my vehicle."

"Really?" Apparently this Sarge was small in stature. And antisocial. Oh, well. So long as he was good at his job, she didn't care.

"Come meet him."

She walked with Cliff to his SUV, her curiosity on the rise. Once there, she peered inside the SUV's open passenger side window and was met by two liquid-brown eyes and a lolling tongue.

"He's a dog!"

Cliff opened the door, and the big shepherd piled out.

"Hey, fellow." Without thinking, she went down on her knees and stroked his head. "Are you a good boy?"

He responded by licking her face. She laughed.

"You like dogs," Cliff said, observing her with interest.

"I love them. If my schedule wasn't so hectic, I'd have one. No, two."

"Scarlett doesn't like dogs."

"She's more of a cat person." Ruby ruffled Sarge's neck, burying her fingers in the thick fur. "We're gonna be good friends, you and I."

"I brought his food." Cliff reached into the SUV and removed a bag of kibble and a leash from the floor board. Also a brown paper bag she assumed contained other necessities for Sarge's care, like treats and a water dish.

"Great!" Ruby popped up and started toward the trailer, only to stop short when she noticed Sarge's awkward gait. Shock reverberated through her. "Oh, my God! He's missing a leg."

"He gets along fine without it. Don't worry. It won't stop him if Crowley or anyone else uninvited shows their face."

She recalled Cliff's earlier remark. "Sarge is a police dog."

"He served five years with the Reno P.D. K-9 Unit." Cliff waited while Ruby and Sarge climbed the porch steps. "He was injured during a drug raid."

"Poor fellow." Her hand lingered on the dog's head.

"The chief of police awarded him two medals at his retirement ceremony, one for his injury and the other for merit."

"Well deserved!" Something else occurred to Ruby as she pushed through the trailer door. "That's where you worked, too, isn't it? The Reno P.D. Before you were elected sheriff."

"Technically, I was appointed sheriff after my dad retired. The election's this November."

He'd avoided the topic of his police career. Ruby wanted to know more. "Were you one of those K-9 officers?"

"K-9 handlers. And, no, I wasn't."

"Then how did you wind up owning Sarge?"

"I worked Drug Investigations. Sarge and I were on a lot of busts together. During his last one, he saved my life."

"Really! How?"

They wandered toward the tiny kitchen. Cliff deposited the paper bag, kibble and leash on the table.

"We stormed a meth lab. Three of the occupants were apprehended. A fourth was hiding. I didn't see him until it was too late. The perp jumped out from behind a corner and pulled a gun on me. Sarge attacked him."

"Is that how he lost his leg? Was he shot?"

"He fell. The perp fought Sarge off and threw him through a second-story window. He landed on concrete."

Ruby's gaze traveled from the dog to Cliff. Her opinion of both soared. "It's a miracle you survived. Sarge, too."

"His attack gave me the distraction I needed to take the perp down. There was never a question about who Sarge would go home with when the veterinarian released him."

"I should say so."

"He'll protect you, Ruby."

Cliff, she realized with a start, was a fake. The hard exterior he put forth shielded a tender heart. He was good with children, cared about the people he served, and he loved Sarge. Not just because the dog had saved his life.

It was easy to see why her sister had been attracted to him. Ruby wasn't immune, either.

"Do I need to know any special commands?"

"Since his retirement, he's learned to respond to the basics. 'Sit.' 'Stay.' 'Come.'"

"Nothing like 'kill' or 'attack' or 'take the scumbag down'?"

He smiled. "Those commands are in German. Though, 'take the scumbag down' isn't one of them."

"Really?" She was impressed. "German?"

"Police dogs are trained in another language."

"I guess they wouldn't be much good if the criminal could get away by telling them to stay."

"Exactly." Opening the paper bag, he began removing white foam boxes and placing them on the table. Obviously not dog items.

"You brought food?" Sidetracked, Ruby craned her neck for a better look. There was enough for six people.

"Dinner," Cliff said. "From the I Do Café. I wasn't sure how well stocked Scarlett left the refrigerator or if you had a chance to eat lunch."

Something told Ruby he already knew the answers. Scarlett wasn't one for stocking refrigerators, and Ruby's lunch had consisted of a protein bar eaten—she glanced at her watch—six hours ago.

"I can't accept," she said.

"Don't worry about it."

"Let me pay you."

Cliff pretended he hadn't heard her.

Left with little choice, Ruby accepted his generosity with a gracious, "Thank you."

"Let's activate this phone then I'll get out of your hair."

"Wait, you can't go!"

"If you're afraid of being alone, rest assured Sarge will do his job."

"It's not that." She motioned to the table. "You have to join me for dinner."

This time Cliff didn't mask his emotions. Indecision showed clearly in his eyes.

"Please," she said. "You've done so much for me. And there's no way I can eat all this food by myself."

He didn't move.

Just when she thought he'd say no, he removed his cowboy hat and hung it on the back of the nearest chair.

"Sure."

A slight thrill Ruby had no business feeling coursed through her.

Sarge made a wuffling sound and rested his large head on his front paws, his way of saying that his human staying for dinner was as it should be.

WHILE RUBY FRESHENED UP, Cliff ransacked the cabinets and drawers for plates and silverware. He'd observed on more than one occasion that Scarlett did next to nothing to make the place her own. He now realized it was probably because she'd never intended to stay long. As they say, hindsight is twenty-twenty.

What about Ruby?

Was there any reason to ask? She would return to Vegas the moment Crowley ceased being a threat. Possibly sooner, for the arraignment and trial. No way would Crowley plead guilty. Not with his father's attorneys at his disposal.

Back in Vegas, Detective James would oversee Ruby's safety. Cliff's involvement would be at an end.

Strange, he felt more disappointment at the prospect of

not seeing her again than he did her sister. And, yet, he hardly knew Ruby.

"Smells good."

She stood in the entrance to the kitchen. Cliff had been so lost in thought, he failed to notice her. Not like him. In his line of work, a lapse in concentration could cost him his life.

"What did you bring?" She came up beside him.

Her scent, the same floral one he'd detected that morning when he pulled her into his arms, enveloped him, giving him all kinds of ideas. The wrong kind.

"I wasn't sure what you liked. If you were a vegan or anything."

"I'm not." The corners of her mouth lifted ever so slightly. "Though I have the greatest respect for people who are."

Those had to be her clothes she wore, not her sister's. Gone were the jeans and work shirt. In its place, Ruby had donned stretch leggings and a tiny T-shirt that hugged her exquisite curves. He had never appreciated the differences between the two sisters more than at this moment.

"There's pot roast." He opened the first food container. "Salmon and rice, chicken and dumplings and vegetable stew. Also Caesar and fruit salads."

"Let's see if Scarlett left anything to drink." She went over to the refrigerator and surveyed the contents.

"Water's fine."

"Good." Ruby closed the door with her hip, a quart-size milk carton in her hand. "Because this is all I found." She shook the carton to demonstrate it contained only a few drops.

After filling their glasses with water and ice, she sat at the table with Cliff. It occurred to him that on the six dates he and Scarlett went on, they'd always eaten out. Never here or at his house. And while they'd spent one evening together on her couch, they'd done no more than kiss a few times.

She'd been keeping him at arm's length. He knew that now and why.

"Can I have some of each?" Ruby asked, her fork poised midair, her expression hopeful.

"Help yourself."

She dug in, serving herself both pot roast and chicken. Not a vegan in the least, Cliff thought and started with the salmon.

"Tell me about you and Scarlett."

He almost choked on his food. "There isn't much to tell," he said, sipping his water. "We didn't date long. And, obviously, not seriously."

"I'm sorry about that."

"Hardly your fault."

"She and Demitri have been together off and on for three years. Every time I think she's over him, they reconcile."

"You don't like him?"

"He's married to his work. And he's a hothead." Ruby sighed. "But he's also smart and good-looking and can be very charming." She paused, her smile remorseful. "I shouldn't talk about him."

"If you're afraid of rubbing salt in old wounds, don't be. I liked your sister. That's as far as it went."

"You brought her flowers."

Sarge had moved from the rug in front of the sink to the table. He didn't beg, he was too dignified for that. But he did wait patiently for any scraps that might happen his way.

"She was avoiding my calls," Cliff said, slipping the dog a piece of salmon. "I didn't want to show up at the square dance alone. I have a reputation to uphold."

"Sweetheart's most eligible bachelor?" A hint of humor lit her eyes. "Or is it Sweetheart's most notorious bachelor?"

"Neither." He chuckled.

"Can't be most confirmed bachelor. Or else you wouldn't have been dating my sister."

"It was strictly for show."

"Ah, yes. That reputation."

"Exactly."

Had his and Scarlett's conversations ever been this light and easy? Not that he could recall.

"What about before Scarlett? How many women have gone down in the annals of history as Sheriff Dempsey's girlfriend?"

This wasn't a discussion he cared to have. He could admit to falling for the wrong woman. Even that he'd been duped by her. What he hated admitting was how close he'd come to ruining his career.

"Dating a police officer isn't for everyone. The woman has to put up with a lot. Cancelled dates. Late nights. Stress and tension spilling over from the job."

"Difficult or not, I think any woman would be lucky to have you."

His reply was noncommittal.

"Why did you leave the Reno P.D.?"

He was beginning to suspect that Detective James had researched him and mentioned his screwup to Ruby.

"My father retired early." This was a topic he could handle. "My mother's arthritis deteriorated to the extent she needed a walker. There were days she couldn't get out of bed."

"How terrible for her."

"Now they live in Phoenix near a clinic that specializes in cutting-edge treatments."

"You must miss them."

"They come home regularly, and I visited them last Christmas."

"Are the treatments helping her?" Ruby had finished the pot roast and was starting on the chicken.

"She's improved. The dry climate's much kinder to her joints."

"So, you took over for your father."

"Family tradition. Seventh-generation sheriff."

Cliff could have remained with the Reno P.D. In a few months or a year, the incident with Talia would have blown over. Mostly. Instead, he left. Everyone in the department was aware of his history, where he was from, and that his plan was to return one day. No questions were asked.

"The day after my dad announced his retirement, the town council approached me."

"The town council your uncle heads?"

He nodded. "They asked me to accept the appointment for sheriff. Insisted I accept it. If I win the election this coming fall, the position will become permanent."

For the next four years, anyway. Barring any screwups.

He didn't inquire about Ruby's love life. Not that he wasn't interested. It didn't seem appropriate when she was hiding out from a stalker.

Instead, he said, "I'm babysitting my nieces and nephew tomorrow evening while my cousin helps decorate the community center for the dance. Can I talk you into coming along with me?"

"What about the risk? I know you told Sam it was minimal, but I couldn't bear it if anything happened to your family."

"I spoke to Detective James earlier. He's been keeping tabs on Crowley. The man's sticking close to home."

"Still…"

"The best way to throw Crowley off and to protect my family is for you to convince everyone you're your sister."

Her smile faltered. "I suppose helping you babysit is something Scarlett would have done."

"She does like the little rug rats."

"And they no doubt like her." Ruby pushed away the last remaining bites of her dinner. "Scarlett's always been great with kids."

Was that a touch of resentment in her voice? Cliff had pondered the differences between the two sisters all day. How Scarlett was a natural with children and Ruby was anything but.

"Come with me tomorrow. I'll run interference."

"I'm not sure."

"We'll go out for ice cream."

One shoulder lifted slightly. She was weakening.

"I'll bring Sarge," he added. "The kids adore him. You'll hardly notice they're there."

"I'll think about it. Let you know tomorrow."

They finished their meals. While Cliff helped Ruby wrap up the remaining food, he told her about Iva Lynn and her position as part-time deputy. Ruby agreed to go by the station the following morning and introduce herself to Iva Lynn.

When the dishes had been washed, she and Cliff sat back down at the table and he showed her the new disposable phone. Together they programed the speed dial numbers she'd need: Cliff's, Sam's, Iva Lynn's, Detective James's and her sister's.

"No personalized voice-mail recording," he said, selecting the generic one.

She nodded in understanding.

When they were done with the phone, he installed small locks on every window in the trailer. The same kind of locks he'd installed in Maeve's house to deter her children.

"These aren't great," he said, "but they're better than nothing. Tomorrow I'll bring a dead bolt for the front door."

"You're pretty handy for a sheriff."

He noticed she tested each lock after he was done.

"Keep the phone with you at all times," he told her at the door as he was leaving. "Don't so much as go to the bathroom without it."

"I promise."

"It could be your lifeline, Ruby."

"You don't have to tell me twice."

Because she seemed nervous, he added, "Same with Sarge. Don't let him stray more than ten feet from you, except when you let him outside. And don't go out with him."

"What about when I'm at work? He might get in the way."

"Drop him off at the station on your way to the Gold Nugget. Then you can pick him up on your way home. He's used to staying at the station all day with my deputy."

"All right."

He bent down to give the dog a farewell petting. Sarge was taking his assignment seriously and sitting by Ruby's side, ears and eyes alert. "I'm counting on you, boy."

The dog nudged his hand.

Cliff checked his watch. "It's seven-thirty now—"

"I'll call you at eight-thirty," she finished for him. "Maybe sooner. I'm really tired. It's been a long day, and I didn't sleep much last night."

"Good night, Ruby."

"Night." She gripped the phone in one hand. The other one rested on Sarge's head.

"You sure you're going to be okay? I could call Iva Lynn. Ask her to stay with you."

"I'll be fine."

He drove away wishing there had been more conviction in her voice and more he could do for her. Ruby was resourceful and courageous in a crisis. That didn't mean she wasn't terrified.

With luck, her impersonation of her sister, his precautions and everything they were doing to keep her safe would be for nothing.

Cliff knew better than to count on it.

## Chapter Six

Ruby climbed out of the old pickup truck and surveyed her surroundings. That morning, when she'd dropped off Sarge and met Iva Lynn, the community-center parking lot had been practically deserted. Now, there were more than a dozen vehicles. Volunteers had arrived to decorate the community center for tomorrow night's BBQ and square dance.

At least one more person was going to show up, if she wasn't already here. Cliff's cousin Maeve. And he was babysitting her children. Ruby had begged off joining him, deciding it was for the best even if being in his company gave her a sense of security and aided her cover.

The list of reasons why their relationship needed to remain professional was a long one. Topping it was Crowley. Being at the center of a stalking case wasn't the best time to start a new romantic relationship. And, technically Cliff was Ruby's protector.

Her feelings for him, however, had started to border on *non*professional. The cozy dinner last night. The hug at his vehicle after the trail ride. Her thoughts constantly drifting to him throughout her work day at the ranch. Their phone calls every hour on the hour.

Truthfully, she knew she'd already crossed the line and would head even further into dangerous territory if she didn't put a stop to it right this second.

Luckily, because of his babysitting duties, Cliff wasn't

at the station. Only Iva Lynn. Despite her knowledge of Ruby and Scarlett's ruse, and Cliff's assurance she was a wonderful person and a competent deputy, Ruby was nervous around the older woman. During their introduction that morning, Iva Lynn's narrowed gaze had constantly raked over Ruby until her skin crawled.

Ruby also had her doubts that a sixty-something-year-old woman could do more than place a phone call should Crowley appear. Of course, a phone call could save her life.

She knocked on the station door and was surprised when no one answered. Didn't that Chevy belong to Iva Lynn? Ruby was more surprised that Sarge didn't bark. He was a diligent watchdog, as she'd discovered last night, and raised the alarm at every noise.

When there was no response to a second loud knocking, she tried the doorknob and found it locked. Strange. Iva Lynn was expecting her, or so Cliff had said.

Her imagination went wild. She saw Iva Lynn in trouble. Helpless in the face of Crowley's deranged whims. Walking back to the old pickup truck, Ruby scolded herself for watching too many TV crime shows. Iva Lynn must be out on a call. But, then, why was her Chevy here?

Ruby was just dialing Cliff when she heard barking coming from the fire station. Certain it was Sarge, she began walking in that direction. Sarge barked again, and she followed the noise.

Ruby entered the metal building through an open door large enough to accommodate the fire truck. She was about to call out when she heard a woman speaking in sharp tones. Iva Lynn.

"Stay, Sarge. Sit. Good boy."

From the sound of it, she was standing on the other side of the fire truck. Ruby started forward, only to come to another abrupt halt when a man spoke.

"There's something wrong with Scarlett. She hasn't been

herself the past couple of days. Are she and Cliff on the outs?"

Ruby recognized the voice as belonging to Will Dessaro, trail boss at the Gold Nugget and her immediate supervisor. He also served as a member of the volunteer fire department and was the town's on-call EMT.

"I wouldn't tell you one way or another even if I did know," Iva Lynn said.

"She's acting different."

"Is she doing her job?"

"Yeah, no problem there. Except Sam is sticking to her like gum to a shoe sole. Annie, too, when he's not nearby. And if I didn't know better, I'd say Sam was doing his level best to keep Scarlett away from me."

Ruby's breath caught. If Will suspected something was amiss, it wouldn't be long before others did, too.

She cautioned herself to be extra careful. Not make one single slip.

"I'd leave things alone," Iva Lynn said. "Cliff, and Sam for that matter, will tell you if there's anything you should know."

"I could ask Scarlett. She and I get along well enough."

*No, please!* A confrontation with Scarlett's supervisor could only go badly for Ruby.

"Don't," Iva Lynn blurted.

"So, there is something going on?"

"I'm just saying, if Scarlett and Cliff are having troubles, neither of them will appreciate you sticking your nose in where it doesn't belong."

*Thank you, Iva Lynn.*

Sarge barked again, more urgently this time. Each loud eruption sent a jolt through Ruby.

"Hush, dog," Iva Lynn commanded. "What's gotten into you?"

"That's another thing," Will said. "Why is Scarlett keeping Sarge all of a sudden? She doesn't like dogs."

"That's between her and Cliff."

"But you know why."

"I just do as I'm told. Not my place to question Cliff."

"Well, I'm questioning him. If he and Scarlett are having trouble, he may need a friend."

"Can't stop you, I guess. But in my opinion, I think you should give them some space for a few days. Better yet, a week."

Iva Lynn was a truly loyal employee. Ruby would mention it to Cliff. Also that his pal Will was onto them. Perhaps she and Cliff should do something to throw the trail boss off track. Like her going with Cliff to babysit his nieces and nephew and making sure she let Will know.

Her shoulders slumped. She wasn't going to get out of spending the evening with him after all.

"Speaking of which," Iva Lynn said, "I'd best get back to the station. She's due here any minute."

Fear propelled Ruby into action. She didn't dare get caught cavesdropping.

Whirling, she swiftly fled the station, worried Iva Lynn and Will might hear her. Sarge did. At least his barking covered the echo of her footsteps.

What now?

Only one choice. Stealing herself, she executed an about-face and headed back the way she'd come, praying neither Iva Lynn nor Will noticed her agitated state.

"Hello. Anybody here?" The scared tremor in Ruby's voice was amplified inside the fire station.

"We're here," Iva Lynn hollered.

The next instant, Sarge barreled out from behind the fire truck. Cliff was right. Missing a hind leg didn't hinder him in the slightest. The dog moved at lightning speed. Reaching Ruby, he jumped up and planted his front legs on her chest.

He couldn't, however, sustain the position on one hind leg and nearly knocked her over. She pushed him gently down before they both landed on the floor.

"Whoa there." She averted her face in a useless attempt to avoid his avid kisses. "I missed you, too."

"There you are." Iva Lynn emerged. She looked exactly as she had that morning—not one close-cropped gray hair out of place, and her khaki uniform free of wrinkles.

Will came up behind her. "Hey. Looks like you have a new friend."

Speaking of looks, his was locked on her and filled with suspicion.

Oh, shoot! Scarlett quickly disengaged herself from Sarge and said, "Good boy." Fearing she didn't sound convincing, she stood straight and added, "You know I hate that."

Sarge responded to the reprimand by pressing up against her leg and raising adoring eyes to her. Then, he broke out into a happy pant.

So much for convincing Will she didn't like dogs.

Ruby grasped at straws. "It was Cliff's idea that Sarge and I spend time together. That way, I could get used to him. Seeing as the dog is a big part of his life, and his cousin's children love him…" She shut her mouth, aware she was rambling.

"I'd say you're making progress."

It was difficult bearing up under Will's close scrutiny. "We, um, both are."

Sarge nudged her hand. Ruby ignored him. He did it again, whining when she didn't respond.

"Well, now that you're here," Iva Lynn announced, "I can hit the road. Hugh hates it when I'm late for dinner."

"See you in the morning." Ruby gave Will a wave.

She exited the station as fast as she could without appearing guilty. Sarge and Iva Lynn kept pace. The older woman could move fast, too.

"Thank you for your help," Ruby said when they were a safe distance away from Will.

"Cliff is right. You are the spitting image of your sister." At the door to the sheriff station, Iva Lynn stopped and crossed her arms over her generous middle. "And you can obviously think on your feet. But you're going to have to do a lot better job impersonating Scarlett if you expect to fool the likes of Will and anyone else who knows her."

"Yeah," Ruby murmured. Hadn't she just come to the very same conclusion? "You have a good evening, Iva Lynn."

She was on the phone with Cliff the moment she climbed in the truck, a full fifteen minutes ahead of schedule.

"You're early," he said. "Something wrong?"

"A change of plans. I'm taking your advice." She swallowed. "What time would you like me at your cousin's house?"

RUBY WAS ATTACKED the instant she stepped across the threshold into Cliff's cousin's house. Three missiles, two fast-moving and one toddling, exploded upon impact, bursting into grins and giggles as they grabbed her hands and dragged her into the living room.

The girls spoke so fast and so loud, Ruby had trouble understanding them. Something about watching a DVD. One that was evidently a favorite. The boy was the complete opposite. He spoke hardly at all, and what he did say was mostly gibberish. It seemed to Ruby that he expected her to understand him. His siblings evidently did.

"Pick him up, pick him up," the older girl singsonged.

The younger girl dropped onto the floor and hugged Sarge as if he were a long-lost friend. The dog endured the zealous attention with dignity.

"Should I?" Ruby glanced around for Cliff. Where was he? He must have heard the ringing doorbell.

"Go on," the older girl commanded, "before he starts

crying. He wouldn't stop after Mommy left. Uncle Cliff had to give him a cookie, and we're not supposed to have cookies before dinner."

Ruby gnawed her lower lip. The kid would probably cry anyway. The last child she'd tried to hold had shrieked loud enough to rupture her eardrums.

"Go ahead, pick him up."

She turned at the sound of Cliff's voice. He stood in the entryway, an easy, sexy grin on his face that did funny things to her insides.

"You sure?" she asked.

"He won't break."

"Famous last words."

Ruby hooked her hands under the boy's armpits and lifted him into the air. Criminy, the kid weighed a ton. She balanced him on her hip, which seemed the best place. The kid immediately shoved ten sticky fingers into her hair. Why had she taken down her ponytail?

"Watch it." She tried to angle her head out of his reach. As luck would have it, the kid possessed the arms of a gorilla.

"Kiss, kiss," he cooed and smacked his equally sticky lips.

Was he kidding? A glance at Cliff confirmed he was not.

"Evan has recently discovered he likes kissing girls." Cliff's grin widened.

"Yuck!" the younger niece complained and swiped a fist across her cheek. Funny, she didn't mind dog kisses, which Sarge generously lavished on her.

"Kiss, kiss." Evan's demands intensified.

Ruby presented the side of her face and prepared herself for the sticky onslaught. The kid went straight for her mouth and planted one on her. It was...all right, not as bad as she'd expected. In fact, it was kind of sweet in a weird way.

"Um, thank you."

He giggled. When Ruby tried to put him down, he clung to her with his gorilla arms. "Noo."

"You have a friend," Cliff observed.

"And all it took was one kiss."

"We men are like that."

A shimmer of heat flashed in his eyes. Ruby felt it clear to her toes.

Oh, my! Thank goodness she had Evan in her arms. She used him as a shield between her and Cliff's potent appeal.

"Did you bring the paints?"

Ruby glanced down at the younger girl. Ellie, right? Cliff had told her the children's names when he'd given her directions to the house. Erin, Ellie and Evan, in that order.

"Paints?"

"You promised." Ellie pouted.

"I'm sorry." Ruby silently sought Cliff's help.

He merely shrugged.

Swell. What kind of paints had Scarlett promised? Finger? Watercolor? "Next time," Ruby said.

"But we were gonna paint tonight," Erin complained.

"We can do something else instead."

"What?"

Ruby tried to recall what pastimes had entertained her and Scarlett as children. "Do you have any board games?"

"Candy Land," Ellie shouted with glee.

Erin groaned. "That game is for babies."

"Is not."

"Is, too."

If Erin and Ellie were anything like Ruby and her sister had been, their bickering could last for hours.

"Girls," Cliff said sternly. "No fighting in front of company."

They stopped instantly.

Ruby was impressed.

"You hungry?" he asked as if nothing had happened.

"Yes!" first Ellie, then Erin, squealed.

"I was talking to Scarlett."

"We're having spaghetti," Erin said. "That's all Uncle Cliff knows how to cook. And cookies for dessert. Usually he gets stuff at the café."

Ruby was immediately reminded of the dinner she and Cliff had shared the previous night. He seemed to remember it, too, for the shimmer of heat reappeared in his eyes.

She swallowed nervously. "Spaghetti's good."

"Well let's eat, then." He led the way to the kitchen.

Ruby tried to act as if she'd been here before and not gawk at the many family portraits hanging on the walls. There was one particularly charming photo of all three kids, Cliff and a woman who had to be his cousin. It was a candid shot of them frolicking in the snow. Ruby would have hung it on the wall, too.

"Can I help with anything?" she asked, walking into the kitchen. Evan still balanced on her hip, and she was beginning to think she'd need a crowbar to pry him loose.

"The girls will set the table. That's their job."

Ruby noticed a loaf of French bread on the counter. "I could slice the bread."

"Good luck. I don't think Evan will let you."

Cliff had a point. The toddler had taken a keen interest in her earrings and was fingering her left one.

"I could try," she said.

Evan suddenly lost interest in the earring and started to fuss. When Ruby tried putting him down again. He began to cry in earnest. *Swell.* Her reputation for being lousy with kids was intact.

"What's wrong?" She didn't pose the question to anyone in particular.

Erin answered. "He's hungry."

Ruby had no idea why, but she started bouncing Evan. It appeared to have a soothing effect, so she bounced him harder. He stopped crying and started laughing. Really? That was amazing. What a neat trick.

It lasted an entire minute before Evan started to whimper.

"Why don't you give him a cookie?" Cliff said as he poured the spaghetti into a colander. "It worked the last time."

Her gaze traveled to the counter and the pink pastry box, courtesy of the café. She went over and contemplated the selection. Chocolate chip and oatmeal raisin.

She grabbed her favorite and handed it to Evan. His cherubic face lit up as he took the cookie and aimed it for his mouth.

Disaster avoided. Ruby sighed with satisfaction.

"What are you doing?" Erin demanded, her tone aghast.

Ruby stared at the girl. "Me?"

She charged over and snatched the cookie from Evan's hand. He began to wail.

"Erin!" Cliff dropped the spaghetti filled colander into the sink. It made a terrible racket. "That's enough."

"Uncle Cliff! She gave Evan a chocolate chip cookie." The girl held up the offending object as evidence.

Ellie gasped.

"Oh." Cliff immediately backed down.

"Did I do something wrong?" Ruby was torn between confusion and defending herself. Hadn't Cliff as much as told her to give the boy a cookie?

Erin scowled at her. "You know Evan's allergic to chocolate. The oatmeal cookies are for him."

"I, uh…" God, what had she done? "I wasn't thinking. Is he all right?" She turned Evan's face toward hers. He seemed fine, other than angry about having his treat taken away. But, then, she was no judge.

"Let me see." Cliff took the squalling boy from her. "How much did he have?"

Erin examined the cookie. "One bite. A little bite," she admitted.

"He couldn't have ingested much chocolate. I think he'll be okay. We'll watch him closely for any reaction."

"I feel awful." Ruby clamped a hand to her forehead.

"It was an honest mistake."

For Ruby. Not Scarlett.

The girls huddled together, gawking at her as if she were a stranger. Which she was. "Maybe I should go home."

"Absolutely not." Cliff placed Evan in the highchair. Once the tray was secured, he fixed a bowl of spaghetti and sauce and gave it to Evan. He instantly quieted. Using his hands as utensils, he dug into his meal. "Come on, girls," Cliff said. "Let's sit down. You, too."

Ruby reluctantly did as instructed. While the girls filled their glasses with milk, she poured iced tea from a pitcher for her and Cliff. By then, he'd delivered a large platter of spaghetti to the table, along with the bread and a salad.

Dinner progressed awkwardly for all save Evan, who enjoyed his meal thoroughly. Cliff told them about his day, which included writing old man Seymour a ticket for shooting the crows in his garden with a pellet gun. Something his neighbors didn't appreciate.

"Sorry," Cliff said midway through the meal.

"For what?" Ruby had only eaten half her food, her appetite having deserted her.

He smiled at her and then the girls. "Sorry the board game. Let's play it after dinner."

"Yay!" Ellie extended her hands above her head as if reaching for the stars. A blob of sauce clung to her chin.

"Erin? What do you say?"

She blew out a long breath. "Okay."

"That's my girl."

The tension immediately dissipated, and the meal continued with the girls chatting nonstop.

"You're good," Ruby mouthed to Cliff, then added aloud, "I'll wash the dishes."

"That's Erin's and my job. You and Ellie can change Evan and dress him in his pajamas."

"Change him?" Ruby's eyes widened. "As in his diaper?"

"And wash him up." Cliff was already on his feet, collecting dishes.

Changing a diaper? Could this be happening to her?

"Come on!" Ellie hauled her out of the chair.

At least Ruby wasn't left on her own to wander the house in search of Evan's room. Ellie danced down the hall, stopping and tapping her foot impatiently when Ruby took too long.

The bedroom belonged to a boy, no doubt about it. Cartoon cowboys and horses decorated the walls, bedding and lampshade. Evan waved an arm, gesturing broadly and babbling. Ruby thought she understood a few words. Pony. Ride. The moon.

Wait a minute. Not the moon. The pony at the Gold Nugget was named Mooney. Evan must have ridden her.

"Do you like to ride ponies?" she asked, surprised to hear herself speaking an octave higher than normal.

"Uncle Cliff takes us sometimes."

Ellie, thank goodness, went right to the changing table and grabbed a clean diaper from a drawer. Ruby didn't have to give herself away by asking the location.

Wipes. Ointment. Powder. She'd watched enough TV, understood the mechanics. Surely she could change a baby. It was infinitely harder than she thought possible. Evan squirmed and wriggled and refused to remain still for longer than a second. Divesting him of his pants took forever.

"Well, you're certainly active, little guy," she told him.

Ellie stood next to Ruby. *Right* next to Ruby. And watched her every self-conscious move.

"Why don't you sing to him like you always do?"

Sing to him? Hmm. Sing what?

"You start," Ruby suggested.

Her trick worked. Ellie, it turned out, could carry a decent tune.

"The wheels on the bus go round and round…"

By the third, round and round, Ruby joined in. Evan quieted and stared at her with huge eyes as she fumbled with the changing. Finishing, she stood him up. The new diaper hung limply to one side. Well, it would have to do.

"Where are his pajamas?" she asked without thinking.

Ellie didn't appear to notice the slip and fetched a pair of superhero pajamas draped over the side of the crib. Ruby wrestled Evan out of his shirt and washed his face, neck and hands with another wet wipe. He giggled when she cleaned his ears.

All right, he was kind of adorable. And Ellie was a good assistant. When Ruby complimented her, the girl beamed.

After fixing Evan's pajama top, which Ruby had put on backward, they returned to the kitchen. By then Cliff and Erin had finished washing the dishes.

"We're ready for bed," Ruby announced, proud of herself.

"You've worn him out." Cliff nodded at Evan.

Only then did Ruby realize the boy clung to her, his small head resting on her shoulder, his thumb in his mouth. "Is he asleep?"

"Almost. Here." Cliff handed her a colorful cup with a lid.

"Am I supposed to drink this?"

Ellie laughed. "You're so funny."

"Give it to Evan. Sit down first. In the rocker."

"The rocker?" Did he mean what she thought he did?

He motioned her toward the living room. "Go on."

She could handle this. She would not let the prospect of rocking a two-year-old child paralyze her.

A brief inspection of the living room revealed that the rocking chair was actually a recliner that rocked. She no sooner sat down then Evan lay across her lap and grabbed the cup. She was glad one of them knew the drill.

He drank the milk while she rocked the chair with the ball of her foot. After a moment, Ruby found herself humming a tune. One her mother used to sing to her and Scarlett when they were young. Evan's eyes drifted closed as he drank. He was asleep before the cup was empty.

Ruby gently removed it from his hands and passed it to Erin for safekeeping. She didn't get up, just kept rocking and humming to Evan. Before she knew it, her mouth had curved up into a smile.

"Night, night, little guy." She kissed the top of his head. His hair was the texture of silk. "I'm so glad I met you," she whispered.

What next? Should she carry him to his crib?

A noise drew her attention. Cliff stood in the entryway, his shoulder propped against the wall.

My, oh, my. He was absolutely scrumptious. Even with a dish towel tucked into the waistband of his uniform slacks. And the way his gaze lingered on her, she might have been a newly discovered treasure.

Ruby's heart warmed. Then, it melted.

Suddenly, Erin stormed into the room, the game tucked under her arm. Her glance pinged from Cliff to Ruby and back to Cliff. "I thought we were going to play Sorry."

And just like that, the sizzling awareness between Ruby and Cliff ended. Ruby wondered how marriages survived the constant interruptions from children.

Laying a drowsy Evan in his crib a few minutes later, watching him snuggle with his stuffed teddy bear, she thought her sister might be onto something.

Kids weren't so bad after all. And an interruption or two was a small price to pay for moments like this.

## Chapter Seven

Ruby hadn't been in the kitchen at the Gold Nugget's main house since that first morning when Cliff kissed her. She entered the room in a rush—and discovered eight pairs of eyes fastened on her.

No less than she deserved for being late to the staff meeting. Her reasons were many.

First, she'd overslept. Awaking with a start and a killer tension headache, she'd raced around the trailer in a frenzy, doing barely more than throwing on some clothes and brushing her teeth.

She'd overslept because of arriving home late from Cliff's cousin's. Maeve had refused to let Ruby leave without 'having a chat'. She'd gotten the distinct impression the woman was fishing for information. That, or Ruby was becoming suspicious of everyone and everything.

Like Erin, for instance. The girl was nobody's fool. Neither was Will Dessaro, whose furtive glances Ruby was avidly avoiding from across the kitchen.

Granted, being late to the staff meeting deserved a furtive glance or two.

Another reason for her tardiness was having to drop Sarge off at the sheriff station. The dog had woken her up three times during the night with his barking.

Okay, that wasn't his fault. His job was to alert her to potential danger and keep intruders away. But each time he'd barked, Ruby bolted upright in bed, then tossed and turned before falling back into a fitful slumber.

During those tossing and turning episodes, she'd think of Cliff, not what had caused the noise. There had been no hug when they parted the previous night. He'd simply followed her home, checked out the inside of the trailer while she waited, then waved goodbye before driving off.

That lack of a hug kept playing through her mind over and over. It shouldn't matter, she reminded herself. The attention he paid her was purely for the sake of appearances.

"Is everyone going to the barbeque and square dance tonight?" Sam asked.

He stood by the sink. On the counter beside him the coffee pot emitted gurgling sounds as it spewed the last drops of a fresh pot.

Ruby eyed the coffee with envy. She wanted a cup. Wanted it with the desperation of a desert wanderer craving water. Instead, she squeezed into the only vacant seat.

The hands of almost everyone in the room shot up in response to Sam's question.

The woman sitting beside Ruby nudged her in the side. "Aren't you going to the dance with Cliff?"

"Oh, yeah." Ruby raised her hand, too.

Fiona. That was the woman's name. She was Sam's mother-in-law as well as head cook and guest relations manager. Ruby's gaze took in the rest of the employees. She silently repeated their names and positions at the ranch. Her third day on the job, and she was still a little unclear.

"Good." Sam smiled. "There'll be no trail rides after 1:00 p.m. and no evening meal served in the dining hall. Any of the guests not attending the dinner and square dance are on their own. Quitting time will be three o'clock so you all can head home early and get prettied up."

Prettied up? Ruby suppressed a sigh. All the hours she'd spent last night thinking about Cliff, not once did she consider what to wear to the dance. She hadn't brought anything suitable along. Maybe Scarlett had something in her closet.

She could call and ask. As of yesterday when they'd talked, Scarlett was in love with Demitri and dreading coming home next week. Ruby hoped her sister didn't do anything rash and impulsive. It wouldn't be the first time.

Then again, who was she to talk? Wasn't she right this minute impersonating Scarlett?

"I want you all to have fun," Sam continued. "You certainly deserve it. But remember, you're representing the Gold Nugget. Conduct yourselves accordingly."

Luis became the center of attention and the brunt of several jokes. Apparently he'd overindulged at the last cookout and hay ride.

"Now, for an update on the Mega Weekend of Weddings." Sam picked up a clipboard and pen from the counter. "As of yesterday, the ranch is booked almost to capacity."

"That's great," someone said.

"For us. Not for the rest of the town, unfortunately. According to the mayor, registration is only about half of what they'd hoped for. Fifty-three couples. Mayor Dempsey's trying to generate more publicity and has invited TV stations from Reno, Carson and Vegas to Sweetheart hoping they'll do a story."

He continued for several minutes, informing the employees on their expected duties. Ruby paid minimal attention. She wouldn't be here in five weeks. Scarlett would. Hopefully, she added.

At the mention of her sister's name, Ruby was suddenly all ears.

"I'm sorry." She looked at Sam. "Did you say something?" Dang it. She should have been listening instead of daydreaming. Once more, all eyes were on her.

"You can drive a buggy, right?" he asked.

She'd never in her life driven a buggy. Scarlett, however,

had spent a year working at Hickory Farms. One of her jobs had been giving wagon rides.

"Um, yes. I can drive a buggy." A bad feeling lodged in the pit of her stomach.

"Good. We'll be hosting our first guest wedding here at the Gold Nugget since we reopened. And it's going to be a traditional cowboy wedding. The groom and groomsmen will ride up on horseback. The bride and her maids will arrive in the buggy. A makeshift altar will be set up on the west hill. The ceremony will take place right at sunset."

"How nice!" Fiona exclaimed and clasped her hands together.

"The wedding is Memorial Day weekend."

Groans filled the room.

"I realize it's short notice, but we didn't want to turn them down for obvious reasons. It goes without saying we have a lot of preparation ahead of us. And we're going to need several run-throughs to perfect the timing of the riders and the buggy. Will." He nodded at the trail boss. "You're in charge of the horses. Scarlett, you're in charge of the buggy. Talk to me or Will on any repairs."

"Okay." Ruby's headache intensified. This was *so* not going to work out for her.

"Now, about the rodeo and gymkhana a week from Saturday." Sam moved on to the next topic without drawing a breath. "There's been a change in assignments."

Ruby had heard mention of the gymkhana from Luis and the stable hand, a high school student who worked afternoons and on the weekends. It was a fun family day for both ranch guests and people from town. There would be calf roping, team penning, barrel racing and horseback relay races. The kids would have their own little buckaroo rodeo, the highlight of which was mutton busting.

Ruby couldn't imagine what parent in their right mind

would allow their child to ride a sheep. Wasn't there a law against it?

Her job, or Scarlett's, actually, was to help with the horses and calves. Again, she doubted she'd be here. Crowley's arraignment was scheduled for this coming Wednesday. And Scarlett was due to return.

One way or the other, Ruby would be gone by then or the next day. But she supposed she could help out before then.

"Scarlett." Sam consulted his clipboard. "I'm putting you in charge of the mutton busting."

"You're kidding!" The words popped out before she could stop them.

"Is something wrong?" He set the clipboard down and crossed his arms. "You told me when I hired you that you have experience with mutton busting."

"Well, yes," Ruby answered meekly, silently cursing her sister. "It's just been a while."

"You can practice with my kids."

"Mine, too," another employee volunteered.

"Okay." She smiled, feeling anything but reassured. Scarlett could not get home fast enough.

The meeting broke up not long after. Ruby made straight for the barn, ignoring the curious stares that followed her and skipping the coffee she longed for. She'd been taken off trail rides again and put on chore duty, which was fine with her. She didn't like the idea of putting the guests in danger should Crowley appear. Better to hide out in the barn.

Sugar Pie and Mooney greeted her with nickers and pricked ears. In the past three days, the old mare and pony had come to expect a petting and treat from Ruby. She didn't disappoint them and pulled two carrots she'd grabbed earlier from her back pocket.

Mooney's thrush was greatly improved, thanks to Sam's daughter's diligent care. Good thing. She was a hit with the younger guests and frequently requested for trail rides.

Sugar Pie was another story. She'd developed an eye infection several months ago that kept returning despite constant treatment. Her advanced age didn't help her ability to fight it off.

Twice each day, Ruby flushed the mare's eyes with water and applied an ointment. When she was done, she exercised the mare by walking her around the grounds.

"Poor girl," she crooned and entered the stall. Mindful of the mare's sensitive eyes, she gently haltered her. "Wish you were better."

If Ruby could accomplish one thing during her week at the Gold Nugget, she wanted it to be getting Sugar Pie over her infection.

She led the mare outside to the wash rack beside the barn. Sugar Pie put up no resistance. Ruby suspected the cool water soothed the mare's painful eyes. She was just finishing up when her cell phone beeped an alarm.

Time to call Cliff. She'd found it easier to set an hourly reminder rather than miss his call and be scolded.

"It's me," she said without preamble when he answered. "Are you busy?"

The last time she'd called he'd been in the middle of a dispute between two ranchers, one with cows and the other with an amorous bull that kept pushing down the fence separating their pastures.

"Just trying to find the owner of an illegally parked car," he said. "Any problems?"

"Yes, and no."

"Tell me." Cliff's tone became brusque.

"It's not Crowley. Don't worry." Ruby wished she'd kept her mouth shut. Well, too late now. "At the staff meeting this morning, Sam assigned me—Scarlett—two new job duties."

"What?"

"The ranch is hosting a wedding in three weeks. I have to drive the bride and her maids up to the alter in a buggy.

Then, he put me in charge of mutton busting at the gymkhana."

"I see."

"Little kids. Sheep. Me in charge. It's a recipe for disaster."

"Ruby, relax."

How could she? "I realize I won't be here for either event. Scarlett will. But there's all this practice and preparation. I don't know the first thing about driving a buggy. The same goes for sheep and kids riding them." Her chin dropped to her chest. "This was such a stupid idea."

"I told Sam earlier I'll help you."

"You can drive a buggy?"

"What do you think?"

Of course he could.

"I don't suppose there's any point in me asking whether you have experience with mutton busting."

"Nope." Was he laughing at her? Probably. "According to my nieces, I'm an expert."

"Why did I even bring it up?"

"You'll do great, Ruby. We'll handle it."

*We.* He was including himself. They'd be spending even more time together.

"Let's talk more about it tonight at the square dance," he said.

"Okay. I need to go. Call you in an hour."

She couldn't lie to herself. His help was what she'd wanted all along. She told herself the reason was because of Crowley and the danger he presented.

The anticipation she felt at the prospect of seeing Cliff tonight made a liar out of her.

EVERY OTHER TIME Cliff had visited the trailer since Ruby's arrival, he'd used her key and gone in ahead of her. This time, he waited at the door and knocked. Sarge's responding bark came instantaneously. Shortly after that, the door opened and Ruby stood before him, Sarge plastered to her side.

She was a vision. The flowered dress she wore fit as if she'd been sewn into it, and her silky brown hair fell in loose waves about her face.

Cliff swallowed the *wow* he'd been about to exclaim and cleared his throat instead. "How you doing?"

"A bit frazzled and running late."

"Take your time." He stepped inside, content with the chance to look at her some more.

"This is Scarlett's one dress. I hope it's okay."

"It's fine." More like drop-dead gorgeous.

Sarge nudged his hand, vying for attention. Cliff had little to spare for the dog. Especially when Ruby sat on the worn couch in order to buckle the slinky sandals she wore. He couldn't pry his glance away if he tried.

Long, toned legs. Slim ankles. Painted toenails. Who knew she'd been hiding those inside her boots? His imagination ran wild, envisioning other, equally delightful, discoveries.

She popped up from the couch. Cliff released his breath.

"Let me grab my purse in the bedroom, and I'll be right back.

*Thank you,* he thought as she sashayed down the narrow hallway.

Sarge whined.

"I know, boy." Cliff patted the dog's head. "I'll be careful."

Ruby emerged a few minutes later. She'd applied lipstick while she was gone. Cliff wanted nothing more than to kiss off every trace of the pretty peach color.

Sarge whined again, Cliff was sure in sympathy. Keeping his hands to himself tonight wasn't going to be easy.

"Ready?" she asked, flashing him a nervous smile.

"Absolutely." Was she feeling the sparks, too?

At the door, she flipped on the porch light. "I just let Sarge out a few minutes ago, so he's fine."

Cliff watched while she locked the door and engaged the new dead bolt he'd installed yesterday. At the SUV, he held open the passenger side door, enjoying the view as she climbed in and tugged on the hem of her dress.

"You look nice," she said when they were on the road. "I haven't seen you out of uniform before."

He cemented his teeth together. Responding to that remark in his current frame of mind would only lead to trouble.

"I'm off duty for the night."

"As the only sheriff in town, I'm surprised you're ever off duty."

"Hopefully, a call won't come in." Dragging himself away from her would be torture.

Loud voices and laughter carried across the community center parking lot as Cliff and Ruby strolled toward the entrance. He didn't take her hand, not trusting himself to stop there.

Heads turned when they walked inside. Cliff believed it was because of Ruby's knockout appearance. He did take her hand after noticing several appreciative male glances cast in her direction. She was with him tonight. Make no mistake.

A band consisting of guitar, banjo and fiddle players set up on the small stage at the front of the room. The aroma of barbequing chicken and hamburgers drifted in from the cookers outside. Linen-covered tables had been arranged end to end near the kitchen and were laden with side dishes and desserts.

Children darted to and fro, friends mingled and couples, young and old, sat close together and smiled fondly at one another.

"Maeve and my aunt are over there." Cliff indicated a

dining table to their right. "Do you mind if we sit with them?"

"Um, sure."

The note of tension in her voice was discernible even over the noisy din. "You can do this, Ruby."

"Scarlett," she said softly. "Remember?"

"Right." The way she looked tonight, he'd have trouble remembering his own name, much less hers. "There's bottled wine coolers and beer over there. If you're inclined."

"Are you having any?"

"One beer's my limit."

"Same here."

They made their way to the beverage station, Cliff returning a dozen hellos and howdys. He selected two beers from the ice chest and left a donation in the money basket. Unscrewing the cap on the first bottle, he handed it to Ruby.

She raised the beer to her lips and took a sip. Cliff stared. And stared.

"Something wrong?" she dabbed delicately at the corner of her mouth.

"Nothing." Nothing an hour alone in the dark with her wouldn't fix.

"I haven't square danced since I was in grade school." Her glance wandered to the large empty area in front of the stage that had been cleared for dancing.

"Can't say I've done it recently, either."

"But more recently than grade school, I'm sure." Her fingers sifted through that mink-colored hair and lifted it off her smooth neck.

Did she have any idea how she looked?

Cliff guzzled half his beer in one swig. He was quite certain he'd never been out with a sexier woman.

Except this wasn't a date. Not really.

He finished the rest of his beer rather than reach for her.

The line he shouldn't, *couldn't* cross was becoming blurrier by the second. Slamming back a beer hadn't helped.

"Let's sit." He escorted her across the room to the table where his family sat. With them around, he'd be forced to behave.

"Hi, Scarlett. Cliff." Maeve greeted them warmly and patted the empty folding chair beside her. "Have a seat. We were just beginning to wonder about you." She smiled up at Ruby. "That's a great dress."

"Thank you," Ruby muttered. Left with no choice, she sat next to Cliff's cousin, clutching her purse self-consciously in her lap.

Cliff slid into the seat across from her. "Where are Erin and Ellie?"

"Playing with Sam and Annie's girls." Maeve wrestled with Evan, who, at the sight of Ruby, tried to launch himself from his mother's lap into hers. "Sorry," Maeve apologized when Evan squealed.

"It's all right."

To Cliff's astonishment, Ruby set her purse on the table and opened her arms. "I can hold him if you want."

"You sure?"

"Hiya, handsome," she said in response.

Evan toppled head first into her lap. Ruby didn't object when he pushed upright, wrapped his arms around her neck and planted a kiss on her mouth. Ruby laughed and used her fingertip to wipe a lipstick smear off his lips. "Look what you've done."

For the first time in his life, Cliff was jealous of a two-year-old.

He caught his aunt looking at him and grinning knowingly. Was he that transparent? Better get a grip on himself and fast.

With the help of Evan, Ruby relaxed, and conversation flowed. Cliff's aunt was eager to update everyone about the

Mega Weekend of Weddings. Her persistence had finally paid off. A TV reporter from a Reno station was coming out the following Wednesday and two more from Vegas the week after. Three new couples had registered, bringing the total to fifty-six.

She kept shooting Cliff glances, as if to say he could bring the total to fifty-seven. A brusque head shake from him didn't dissuade her.

The loudspeaker abruptly crackled to life and Cliff's uncle, who was head of the town council, boomed, "Evening, folks. Thank you all for coming. We've got quite a crowd." After several mandatory announcements about the location of trash receptacles, shoes being required on the dance floor and thanking the decorating committee for doing such a stellar job, he said, "Dinner will start in ten minutes. Dancing commences at seven, so be ready to grab your partner and do-si-do."

"I'd best take this young man to the restroom for a hosing down before we eat." Maeve removed Evan from Ruby's lap. "For the life of me, I can't figure out how he gets so dirty." She looked around. "Where are the girls? Sam and Annie must have had their fill by now."

Evan resented leaving Ruby's lap and squawked loudly. Cliff commiserated.

"I'll go with you." His aunt sprang from her chair. "I could use with some freshening up. Scarlett, why don't you join us?"

Her intentions were about as subtle as an elephant trumpeting.

"Um…" Ruby sought out Cliff.

He nodded reassuringly. "I'll hold down the fort."

The trio of women and one fussy little boy navigated their way through a maze of people and tables. Cliff hoped his aunt behaved. Ruby could handle herself, but his aunt gave new meaning to the word *pushy*.

"Hey, pal."

Cliff felt a firm hand clapping his shoulder and turned. Will sank into the seat Ruby had just vacated.

"Where's Miranda?" Cliff asked.

Will had married his love this past March, to the delight of the entire town. Miranda owned and operated Harmony House, an elder-care group home. She would soon be opening a second Harmony House, this one for special-needs foster children.

"Over there."

Cliff followed his friend's gaze. The four senior residents currently in Miranda's care were seated at a table. She fussed over them with the dedication of a mother hen. He imagined she took care of Will with the same dedication.

"You're a lucky man," he said.

"Tell me about it." Will broke into a huge grin. "Miranda's pregnant."

Cliff grabbed Will's hand and gave it an enthusiastic shake. "No fooling!"

"We found out a few weeks ago. She wanted to wait before telling anyone. Make sure everything was okay and that the baby's healthy." He grinned again. "Doc says it is."

"Congratulations."

Cliff's elation at his friend's good fortune couldn't be more genuine. Few folks knew that Will had struggled with posttraumatic stress disorder for years after his parents' deaths. He'd overcome it only with Miranda's help. No one more than him deserved to be happy.

"Thanks." He paused, his smile dimming. "Hey, look. There's something I wanted to talk to you about before Scarlett gets back."

"What's that?" Cliff guessed Will's concerns had something to do with the volunteer fire department or his duties as the town's EMT.

"She's been acting funny lately."

Okay, not about the fire department. "How so?"

Of course, Cliff knew exactly *how so*. He didn't mention that to Will, however.

"Can't pinpoint it exactly. She seems distracted a lot. Kind of nervous. Asks a lot of strange questions."

"Strange?"

"About things she and I discussed last week. Or where equipment is. Equipment she was the last to use. And Sam's acting funny, too, where she's concerned. He's pulled her off of the trail rides. And when I needed her to drive into town to pick up some horse pellets at the feed store, he told me to send Luis instead."

"Huh."

"It's none of my business, but you and I are friends. If the two of you are having a fight—"

"We're not fighting," Cliff said in a tone meant to shut Will down. It did.

"All right." He scooted his chair back and rose to leave. "Like I said, none of my business."

"Hold on a minute. It's not that."

Will sat back down.

Cliff debated what to say. Ruby didn't need her boss analyzing her every move. The right answer from him would prevent that. "She's having some family issues. A problem with her sister."

Will appeared almost hurt. "Why didn't she tell me?"

"It's personal."

"But she told Sam."

"She didn't have a choice."

"I'm on her side, Cliff. I happen to think she's a good wrangler."

"I'll talk to her about including you." Actually, Cliff didn't think it was a bad idea at all. Especially if Crowley or one of his hired men showed up.

"If you're sure."

Cliff caught sight of Ruby, his aunt, Maeve and Evan returning from the "hosing down" and "freshening up". Ruby's features were drawn tight. Great. His aunt and probably Maeve, too, must have drilled her for information.

"This problem of Scarlett's, it's going to resolve itself soon. Hopefully in a week or two. Can you cut her a little slack until then?"

"Sure."

"And congratulations again," Cliff said as the trio of women and one surly toddler approached. "That's great news."

"What's great news?" Cliff's aunt asked.

It was exactly the distraction Cliff had hoped for. The moment Will said that his wife was pregnant, Cliff's aunt and cousin were all over him, clamoring for details.

He tilted his head toward the serving tables and said to Ruby, "Why don't we get in line?"

She was beside him in a flash.

"We'll be along in a minute," his aunt called after them.

Cliff was counting on it being several minutes. "Were they tough on you?"

"Not so much tough as blunt." She peered at him through lowered lashes. "Your aunt really wants you to get married."

"She does have that idea."

"According to her, she gets that idea from you."

He didn't have an answer for Ruby. Being a husband and father were indeed in his future plans.

"Is that why you were pursuing my sister?"

The topic was a sticky one for Cliff. "I liked your sister, but we'd only dated a few weeks. It was way too early to consider marriage."

"I'm sorry about Demitri."

"All for the best."

"What are you going to do when she comes back? You can't keep pretending…"

Was Ruby really curious about her sister? Or did she want to know what Cliff would do when *she* left?

They fell into line behind the manager of the general store and his wife. Cliff dipped his head close to Ruby's so as not to be overheard. "She and I will just have to break up."

"And if she and Demitri have another falling out? You and Scarlett could pick up where you left off."

Not going to happen. Scarlett wasn't the one for Cliff, regardless of Demitri. He'd learned that much these past few days.

Neither was Ruby the one for him. Not while she was under his protection and her safety threatened.

That didn't change how much he wanted her, however. Sitting near her, dancing with her—it was going to be a long night.

## Chapter Eight

"Did you have a good time?"

Ruby smiled at Cliff. "I did." In fact, she had a far better time than she'd anticipated.

"Told you, square dancing isn't that hard."

"It's not exactly easy, either."

"But after a few 'swing your partners,' you got the hang of it."

What would it be like to dance with Cliff in a honky-tonk? Where they could two-step or, better yet, slow dance? He hadn't held her tonight except to promenade.

She could imagine their fingers linked. His other hand pressed into the small of her back. Their bodies swaying in rhythm to the music.

Whoa! This was not the direction her thoughts should be going in.

They were walking from his SUV to her trailer. His question had broken a lull that had stretched during the entire drive home. Strange. They'd had no trouble talking all evening, except for that one little bump when Cliff's aunt and cousin had cornered her in the restroom.

She wasn't mad. They cared about him. *Everyone* in town cared about him. That much had been abundantly clear. Cliff wasn't just their sheriff, he was their friend. They wanted him to be happy. And if Scarlett made him happy, they would gladly welcome her into their fold.

Only Ruby wasn't her sister, and she wasn't Sheriff Dempsey's girlfriend. She was a fraud. A stranger who was planning on leaving soon.

"Key?" He held out his hand.

"Right." She removed it from her purse and gave it to him.

On the other side of the door, Sarge barked, then whimpered with excitement when Cliff inserted the key and turned the knob.

"Wait here," he instructed.

"Of course." After three days, she was used to this.

Sarge bounded outside the moment the door was opened. After a well-deserved petting, he trotted off to investigate the nearby trees and bushes while Cliff searched the trailer.

"All clear," he called from inside.

"Here, Sarge." Ruby clapped her hands.

The dog was slow to respond. He stood staring off into a darkened stand of ponderosa pines on the corner of the property.

Cliff came to the door. "Something wrong?"

"Just Sarge. Maybe he's spotted a squirrel or something."

Cliff's brows formed a deep V. Just as he shoved past Ruby, Sarge suddenly turned and returned to the trailer, his tongue lolling in a silly dog grin.

"Guess it was a squirrel after all," she said.

"Yeah." Cliff's tone was skeptical. "Come inside."

He followed close on her heels.

"You staying?" she asked.

"Just for a few minutes."

"I'm fine, Cliff." She tossed her purse on the coffee table. "You can leave."

"I will. Soon."

Was it possible he didn't want to go?

It was entirely possible *she* didn't want *him* to go.

"Can I get you something?" She wasn't thinking of water.

Neither was he. Heat flared in his eyes. "I'm okay."

She liked it when he showed emotion. Liked it a lot.

Seconds ticked by. Neither of them moved.

This was stupid, Ruby thought. Any relationship they had was doomed from the start. Her home was in Vegas. His in Sweetheart, three hours away. She was evading a stalker and would probably be a material witness in his upcoming trial. One of them needed to be the adult.

"I'm pretty sure the coast is clear," she said.

"You're right." He inched slowly away.

She buried her frustration. What did she expect? For him to sweep her into his arms? Hadn't she just admitted the pointlessness of that?

"Call me before you go to bed," he instructed.

"Not necessary. I'm heading straight there."

"Call me anyway."

Because he wanted to talk to her as she was slipping beneath the covers?

He hesitated on the porch. "I had a nice time tonight."

Her heart skipped. That was the kind of remark a man made to a woman at the end of a real date. Not a pretend one.

"Me, too."

"Yeah?"

"I did." She gazed up at him, wondering what his touch would feel like.

He was obviously adept at mind reading for he brushed a lock of hair from her face.

Ruby's skin tingled in the wake of his fingers. Unable to resist, she closed her eyes. Then, it happened. His lips brushed hers.

Nice. Sweet. Tender. So different from the harsh, cold kiss of that first day.

He drew back, and Ruby opened her eyes. Sadly, the moment was over.

Only it wasn't over. The next instant, Cliff grabbed her

by both shoulders and hauled her up onto the tips of her toes. Their faces were inches apart.

"Is this for show, too, Cliff?" The intensity of her voice surprised her, considering how utterly weak she felt. "Because I doubt anyone's watching."

"Hell, no."

His mouth covered hers in a kiss that rivaled all others. Ruby surrendered to the power of it. The fire. The raw passion. This was no pretense. Cliff was kissing her. *Ruby*. With a desire that left no doubt she was at the center of his every fantasy.

Rocking against him, she reveled in the sensation of his solid frame and the unmistakable response to her he couldn't hide. This was how a man and woman were meant to fit together. Melding perfectly, like two halves to a whole.

Sounds escaped them both. A low groan from him, a thready sigh from her. Cliff's arms circled her, creating a lock from which there was no escape. Ruby's hands ventured on their own quest, climbing his arms to his broad shoulders, then upward to cradle his cheeks. The slight bristle of his five-o'clock shadow tickled her palms.

She sighed again and pulled him deeper into the kiss. After that, Cliff took control, and his skills didn't disappoint.

The insanity—she could think of it as nothing else—ended too soon. He, and not she, had come to his senses first.

"I shouldn't have done that," he said, his breathing harsh.

"You're right." Her head felt light. The result of an intoxicating kiss from an utterly incredible man.

"I won't let it happen again."

*Too, too bad.* "That's probably wise."

"Call me before you go to bed," was all he said before taking his leave.

As if she could go to sleep after the last ten minutes.

Ruby locked the door, leaned her back against it and

smiled ridiculously wide. Mistake or not, kissing Cliff had been mind-boggling. Earth-shattering. And so worth it.

She went to the window and eased back the curtain. Cliff was only just leaving. She watched until the red taillights of his SUV disappeared completely.

"Good night, Cliff," she said to herself. "Thank you for the lovely time."

In the hall, Sarge blocked her path. He wore an inscrutable expression on his face.

"What are you staring at?"

If dogs could roll their eyes, Sarge would.

"It was one kiss." One phenomenal kiss. "He said it wouldn't happen again."

She'd hardly reached her bedroom when her cell phone rang. Cliff! He hadn't waited for her.

Ruby returned to the coffee table and dug the phone out of her purse with shaking fingers.

Not Cliff. Rather, a number she didn't recognize. Her heart went from fluttering to racing.

She wasn't answering. Not after the last time. Clutching the phone in her suddenly damp palm, she let the call go to voice mail and waited for the ding notifying her of a message. The phone screamed silence.

Knowing it was useless, she checked for a message anyway. A droning female voice informed her there were none.

"It was just a misdial, right?"

Sarge didn't answer her. He was too busy sniffing at the door.

"What is it? Another squirrel?"

A low but lethal growl emanated from the dog's throat.

Ruby didn't think dogs growled at squirrels. "Sarge?"

He stood on his one hind leg and propped his front paws on the door, then started barking in earnest. Ruby jerked and nearly dropped her phone. She was no longer nervous but downright scared.

Starting for the window, she stopped in midstep. Was that prudent? Not with the lights on. If someone was out there watching her, they would see her through the window. Unless she turned off the light.

Cliff's warning reverberated in her head. Light was her best defense.

She should call him. And tell him what exactly? That Sarge was barking at the door. Knowing Cliff, he'd come rushing back, only to find nothing out of the ordinary.

Seconds later, the dog quieted. Sitting, then falling onto his side, he scratched his neck with his one hind leg. When he was done, he stood and shook from head to tail, completely unconcerned.

Cliff was definitely going to get his wish. Ruby was calling him before she went to bed.

She waited a while longer. When nothing more transpired, she went to the kitchen and turned on the light there. The bedroom was next. She wasn't satisfied until the trailer was lit up like the Vegas strip. Climbing into bed, she invited Sarge to sleep with her. Stuffing pillows behind her back, she pressed the speed dial for Cliff's number.

"Hey."

"Everything okay?" he asked.

"I guess."

"You sound upset."

Was he that attuned to her already? "Sarge started barking after you left, but then he stopped."

"And now?"

"He's sleeping."

"I'll be right there."

Just what she'd expected him to say. "Cliff, you can't come running every time Sarge barks."

"I won't disturb you."

Since there was no stopping him, she simply said, "Good night. I'll talk to you in the morning."

She lay awake for the next ten minutes, listening for the rumble of Cliff's vehicle. True to his word, he didn't knock on her door and left soon after. Clearly, he'd found nothing. Sarge was just responding to a harmless noise as dogs are apt to do.

The reassurances didn't help. Sleep evaded Ruby for hours. Crowley's arraignment couldn't come soon enough.

What would she do? How would she protect herself, once she'd returned home and Cliff was in Sweetheart?

THE SOUND OF BLEATING SHEEP reached Cliff's ears long before the small rodeo arena came into view. Sarge sprang instantly to life. Ears pricked, eyes alert, his hobble smoothed into a fast trot. This was hardly his first interaction with livestock, and the loss of a limb wouldn't hinder his enjoyment.

Fifty feet short of the arena, Cliff stopped to observe Ruby.

Hatless, long hanks of hair falling loose from her ponytail, and every inch of her covered in grime, she chased a herd of six adult ewes in circles. In this game of tag, the ewes were clearly ahead. While Ruby stopped to rest, visibly struggling to catch her breath, the formerly fleet-footed sheep stood bunched together, glaring at her and bleating insults.

Sarge whined in eager anticipation.

"*Sitz,* boy. *Bleib.*"

The dog sat, but every muscle strummed with excitement. His police training was all but set aside as the herding instinct encoded in his DNA took over.

"No worries," Cliff assured the dog. "You'll have your chance. She won't get those sheep rounded up without you."

From what he could tell, Ruby was attempting to wrangle a sheep, or multiple sheep, into the bucking chute.

In the sport of mutton busting, a child, usually around the age of three to six, was placed on top of the sheep and instructed to hold tight. The sheep was then released to run the length of the arena, and the child's ride was timed. Sort of like bull or bronc riding, only on a smaller scale and considerably less dangerous.

Winners were determined by the longest ride and awarded a ribbon. Skill and technique didn't count. Generally, all the participants received some sort of prize for having the courage to compete. They'd earn it, too. Mutton busting was a tough sport, and every rider eventually landed face first in the dirt. The kids, however, loved it. For the most part.

Trying and failing again to drive even one sheep into the bucking chute, Ruby braced her hands on her knees and burst out laughing.

Cliff chuckled along with her. She might be in over her head when it came to herding sheep, but she was having fun and not taking herself seriously. He liked that about her.

He liked a lot of things about her. Too many for his own good.

It was a relief to see her happy. He'd worried about her the past few days. While they'd talked every hour, they hadn't seen each other since the night of the square dance. It was now Monday afternoon. Cliff had decided that, in light of their kiss, a little distance might be in their best interests.

What he hadn't counted on was how much he'd missed her. The sight of her now was like emerging from a dark cave into full sunlight. Their time apart had done nothing to temper his desire for her.

In his place, Cliff had recruited Sam to escort Ruby home from work on Saturday and Iva Lynn to drop by on Sunday, Ruby's day off. Cliff continued driving past the trailer on rounds, verifying that all was well. He'd glimpsed her and Sarge only once. She'd waved, and Cliff had cursed under his breath.

According to Iva Lynn, his dog wasn't happy about being

dropped off at the station and had moped all morning. Apparently, he was settling in nicely with Ruby.

And she, Cliff thought as he continued watching her, was settling in nicely to life as a wrangler. Sarge would be lonely when she left.

Cliff, too.

Ruby finally managed to corner one ewe, only to have it break loose at the last second. This could go on all afternoon.

Cliff approached the arena and opened the gate. "Away, Sarge," he commanded.

Yipping, the dog sprinted across the arena toward the sheep, his gait slightly unnatural but incredibly fast. In a matter of seconds, he had the six ewes standing shoulder to shoulder and perfectly still.

"Hold," Cliff called out as he walked toward Ruby, confident in his dog's abilities to keep the flock in place.

She stared in amazement, first at Sarge, then Cliff. "Did that just happen?"

He grinned. "When I brought Sarge home after his release, he needed physical therapy and daily exercise. Like some people, I suppose, he was depressed over his injury and the loss of his job. The vet told me to keep him busy. Herding sheep at old man Seymour's place is what we did. I still take him there once a month for a workout."

"You could've told me."

"I could have. But watching you try to herd sheep was fairly entertaining."

She grinned then, too. The worry Cliff had been holding on to dissipated. She wasn't mad at him.

"What now?"

"Watch this." He went over to the pair of chutes and swung the doors wide. He stood by the first one. Here was the part where Sarge really shined.

Whistling shrilly, Cliff issued another command. Sarge

was off in a flash. It took the dog less than two minutes to divide the sheep and herd the first group into a chute. Cliff closed the door behind them. The second group was contained just as quickly. Tongue lolling and wearing his I'm-a-good-dog face, Sarge hop-trotted back to Cliff.

"That'll do, boy." He stroked Sarge's head.

"He's amazing!" Ruby came over and hugged the dog's neck. To Cliff she said, "Please tell me I can use him during the gymkhana."

"He's all yours."

She straightened, her features falling. "I don't know why I said that. I won't be here."

Yet another reminder of her impending departure. The powers that be must be sending Cliff a message.

"You can use Sarge until you leave. For practices."

"Thanks."

Their gazes locked. Was she recalling their kiss? He certainly was. Constantly.

"Speaking of which, can I also borrow your nieces? I need victims. I mean, volunteers."

He laughed. "I'm sure they'll be thrilled."

"Do you know anyone with a small protective vest we can borrow? We already have riding helmets."

"Let me make a call. The problem is getting it here in time."

"I'd offer to drive and pick it up, but I'm thinking you won't allow that, Sheriff Dempsey."

"You are correct."

"What if you came with me?"

"What if we send Luis instead?"

"Okay," she muttered grumpily.

"Are you getting bored?"

"Not with the work. But I wouldn't mind a change of scenery."

Between Cliff and Sam, they'd kept her on a short leash.

Other than the square dance and the trail ride her first day, she hadn't been anywhere except the ranch and the trailer. Even walks with Sarge were discouraged.

"Have you had any other disturbances?" Cliff asked.

"Not since the last one."

"Detective James called. The arraignment is on schedule."

"That's what I hear." She sighed expansively.

"Are you planning on attending?"

Confined in the chutes, the sheep had quieted down. Sarge patrolled back and forth in front of the chutes, primed for action should one of them attempt escape.

Ruby wiped her forearm across her brow, smearing the dirt smudge rather than wiping it off. Cliff considered telling her. He didn't. She looked too cute.

"Probably not," she finally said. "The prosecutor advises against it."

"You want to be there," he guessed.

"I want to see him brought to justice." She shook her head. "Not that my being there matters. Crowley won't plead guilty."

"It could be weeks before the trial starts."

"Or months. His attorneys will use every trick in the book to postpone."

"Maybe you should stay here." He was being selfish.

"If I do, I'll lose my job."

She had to return to Vegas. He doubted the wages she earned as a wrangler were enough to pay the mortgage on her fancy condo.

"Crowley could still be a threat to you after the arraignment."

"I have the order of protection. And Detective James thinks Crowley's attorneys will make sure he stays out of trouble. Besides," Ruby added, "Scarlett's coming home soon."

"Have you talked to her lately?"

"Yesterday. She's miserable about leaving Demitri." Ruby grimaced. "Sorry. Didn't mean to rub salt in the wound."

"I'm over her. I would think you'd figured that out after Saturday night."

Ruby blushed, the bright pink of her cheeks visible through the many layers of dirt. "We should probably talk about…that."

"Not if you don't what to."

"You've been avoiding me."

"We needed space."

"I realize the situation with us isn't ideal." She shoved her hands in her pockets, a nervous gesture he'd learned to recognize. "It's a long drive between here and Vegas."

"Distance isn't the only problem." He wished it was.

"I know." She sighed. "Crowley."

She was right but not for the reason she thought.

"You're under my protection, Ruby."

"You think I'm confusing feeling safe with feeling attraction?"

"No." Was she? "We need to keep our relationship aboveboard." And above reproach. "I need to."

"Is this the 'it's me and not you' speech?"

"I'm sorry. I shouldn't have led you on."

"What aren't you telling me?"

How did she know? "If things were different…"

She turned away. "Now I'm getting the 'if things were different' speech."

This dilemma was his fault. His doing. He brought it on by kissing her. She had good reason to be angry at him. If he leveled with her, she might understand and be less angry.

Cliff made a snap decision. "Let me take you to dinner at the Paydirt."

She snatched her hands from her pockets. "I thought we agreed dating wasn't an option."

"We did. But what I have to say will be easier over a beer and good food."

"It's that terrible?"

He didn't answer her, except to say, "I'll swing by the trailer about six."

## Chapter Nine

Cliff couldn't remember the last time he'd been nervous picking up a woman for dinner. It had nothing to do with the company and everything to do with the upcoming conversation. He hadn't spoken about Talia and his blunder with anyone except his father, and that had been a grueling ordeal.

Tonight would be worse. Cliff had been confident his father's opinion of him wouldn't change significantly. Not so with Ruby.

She was dressed more casually than the night of the square dance—shorts, a flower-print blouse and flats. Cliff had gone home first and swapped his uniform for regular clothes, wanting to send a clear message to anyone watching that he wasn't on duty.

Mondays were far slower at the Paydirt Saloon than weekends, and the sparse crowd reflected it. Cliff and Ruby were able to find a corner booth, away from prying ears, at least, if not prying eyes.

"What's good?" she asked, studying the menu.

"Pretty much everything."

Like the general store and trading post, Cliff had spent a lot of time in this establishment. He wasn't sure which of his great-great-whatever uncles had originally founded the saloon. The last one had left the saloon to Cliff's aunt and the store to her brother, Cliff's uncle.

An interesting choice. Most people might have done the opposite.

That last great uncle had been smart. Cliff's social-butterfly aunt excelled running the saloon and being mayor while his uncle was a natural businessman and an excellent head of the town council.

A waitress met them at their table the moment they were seated. "Can I bring something to wet your whistle?"

"Iced tea, please."

"I'll have a draft ale." After the server left, Cliff asked, "Not drinking?"

Ruby shook her head. "I don't much. Funny, I know. I started out as a cocktail waitress before becoming assistant manager."

No smile. She was nervous, too.

When the waitress returned with their drinks, Ruby ordered the fried-chicken special. It sounded good so Cliff had the same.

"I've been eating a ton since coming here." She patted her flat belly. "I just hope I'm working it off."

He could personally attest to it she was. Ruby's figure turned many a man's head, his included. Which was the reason he'd brought her to a public establishment rather than his house. Less temptation.

"You look like you're struggling with where to start." She rested her folded hands in front of her. "I'm a good listener. It comes with the job."

"I bet you've heard a lot of stories from customers."

"All kinds."

Cliff collected his thoughts over a sip of ale. "If we'd met under any other circumstances, I'd be romantically pursuing you."

"Such as closer to Vegas?"

"Not a crime victim seeking refuge in my town."

"I see."

"While you're here, it's my duty to protect you. I can't compromise that by becoming personally involved."

She stirred sugar into her iced tea. "You were personally involved with someone before?"

Ruby was astute. That probably came with the job, too.

"Her name was Talia Hanks. She was a witness in a case. For over a year, RPD Drug Investigations had been working on bringing down Vladimir Krupin."

"The Russian crime lord?"

"We were closing in on his right-hand man, Niro Unkovsky. Talia worked for him. A secretary in his so-called transport business. We arrested her on an unrelated charge—writing bad checks—and presented her with a deal. Information in exchange for having the charges dropped."

"She was your snitch."

"Our sources reported she was low on the totem pole. A lackey. Not a criminal or an associate of a criminal. Just a nice person who made a couple bad decisions, one of them working for the wrong man. She seemed sincere, wanting to get out of the illegal drug-trafficking trade and change her life for the better."

"You fell in love with her." There was no judgment in Ruby's voice.

"I developed feelings for her. I don't know if it was love or not. I couldn't imagine how such a sweet, sensitive woman got involved with Niro Unkovsky. She fed us information about Vladimir Krupin, the kind we were hoping for, and we were able to build our case. Everything was going great. We were hours away from the bust of the decade."

Cliff paused. A sick feeling formed in the pit of his stomach as he relived the emotions he'd felt when Talia's deception became apparent. Shock and disbelief, then rage and finally, shame.

"What happened?" Ruby asked gently.

"When the SWAT team arrived at Krupin's headquarters, the place had been cleaned out. Every trace of evidence gone. They were onto us. And I was the leak."

"Talia?"

Cliff sipped his ale. Sixteen months later, and he was still paying the price for his acute lapse in judgment.

"She'd been using me the whole time. Turned out, she wasn't just a lackey in Unkovsky's office."

"His mistress?"

"Believe it or not, her mother was. Thirty years ago. She married someone else after the affair ended, which is why we didn't make the connection. When Talia's mother became ill a few years ago, Unkovsky helped pay for her cancer treatment. Then, he gave Talia a job. She was fiercely loyal to him."

"The case falling apart wasn't your fault," Ruby said.

Cliff barked a laugh. "It was *all* my fault."

"She used you."

"She couldn't have used me if I hadn't let her." The disgust he felt at himself still revolted him.

"Is that why you quit the force?" Ruby asked.

"Not entirely." Cliff polished off his beer just as their food arrived, glad for the break. He waited until after the waitress left to continue his story, his emotions again in check. "My dad retired. I was under a lot of pressure to take over for him."

"Do you want to be sheriff of Sweetheart?"

Cliff frequently pondered that same question. "Maybe not at first. But now, I'm glad. The job suits me."

"I think it does, too."

Cliff had thought unburdening his heart to Ruby would diminish his appetite. Instead, he was ravenous and attacked his dinner like a starving man.

Unlike him, Ruby took normal-size bites of her food. "You and I, it's not the same thing as you and Talia."

"Close enough. Neither of us can afford to have my judgment impaired. Your well-being could depend on it."

"You're right." Her expression became melancholy. "Doesn't mean I have to like it."

"I definitely don't like it."

"Thank you for telling me about Talia. I'm sure it was hard for you."

An understatement if ever he'd heard one.

"I want you safe, Ruby. Nothing is more important to me."

"Because you're the sheriff, and it's your duty."

"And because I care about you."

She set her fork down. "If that were so, then why—"

"I can't make the same mistake twice."

A moment passed before she nodded. "I understand."

He hoped she did. Her lackluster response made him wonder.

The remainder of their meal was spent on small talk. Ruby was planning the pony relay races and goat-dressing contest for the gymkhana on Saturday. She was also supposed to start practicing driving the buggy. Cliff offered to come by tomorrow afternoon.

"Are you sure?" she asked. "Given what we just decided?"

"As long as Crowley's out there and you're pretending to be Scarlett, we need to maintain appearances. I'll bring the kids and Sarge. We can work on the relay races after your driving lesson."

"Yippee," she drawled sarcastically.

With the bill settled, they left the Paydirt. During their meal, the sun had set, and they walked outside into a blue-gray twilight. Before long, night would be upon them. They strolled side by side to Cliff's SUV. No hand-holding.

"Thanks for din—" Ruby was cut off by the ringing of her cell phone from inside her purse.

They both stopped, their gazes locking. Memories of Crowley's last call flashed in Cliff's mind.

"Want me to answer it?" he asked.

She checked the display on the simple flip phone, relief relaxing her features. "It's Scarlett." She pressed the phone to her ear. "Hey, sis."

Cliff listened as she talked.

"That's great…No, I'm glad." Ruby paused between responses. "Things are going well." She shot Cliff a glance. "He's fine. Helping me a lot with the gymkhana…Yeah, you did forget to mention that."

He would have liked to send her a wink or casual grin. The kind of exchange between two people on good terms with each other.

He didn't. Their kiss had confused matters enough.

"The ranch is hosting a cowboy wedding. I—you—will drive the bride and her maids to the alter in a buggy." Ruby stopped suddenly. "What are you saying?"

What was Scarlett saying?

"You can't." Ruby looked at Cliff, her mouth drawn tight. "I know, but—" She groaned.

He touched her arm in an offer of support.

"We'll talk later," Ruby said firmly. "I need to go…I don't care." Every response was clipped. "Then I'll call when you get home…Fine. Bye."

She snapped the phone shut. He swore he heard her teeth grinding.

"Problem?"

"My sister only thinks of herself." Ruby tromped the remaining distance to the SUV.

Once they were seated inside, Cliff started the engine. "I take it she's not coming back."

"She wants more time. She's afraid if she leaves Demitri now, all the progress they've made will be for nothing."

"If he really loves her, it won't."

"Exactly!" Ruby crossed her arms in front of her and blew out a breath. "If anything, she should come back to Sweetheart, give Sam a reasonable two-week's notice, then return to San Diego."

"Does she expect you to finish out her two weeks?"

Ruby's angry silence gave him his answer.

"Is that such a bad thing? You said yourself, you weren't sure what you were going to do after the arraignment."

She shot him an astonished look.

"Don't let me be the reason you're rushing to leave," he said.

"It has *nothing* to do with you."

Did she have to emphasize *nothing?*

"I'm going to the arraignment," she abruptly announced.

"Cowley could have you followed from the courthouse."

"He won't. If anything were to happen to me, he'd be the first person the police questioned."

"That's the thing about stalkers. They aren't rational. Their need to dominate overrules their reason. You'd be taking a big chance."

She stared out the windshield. "I'm tired of him ruining my life."

Cliff couldn't argue with her. In a way, that man was ruining Cliff's life, too.

RUBY HAD LEARNED SOMETHING during the past half hour. Six children, two Nubian goats, three horses and a herding dog equaled total and complete chaos.

The animals and youngsters both were running amok in the rodeo arena. Well, Evan wasn't, though he desperately wanted to be with the others. Unfortunately for him, he was trapped in his mother's arms, a state he protested loudly.

"Sorry, baby," Maeve said. She and Evan stood at the arena fence, watching the mayhem. "You're too small, you'll get trampled."

She didn't appear the least bit concerned that her other two offspring were playing perilously close to horses' flying hooves.

Ruby, however, was frantic. The chances these little maniacs were taking, pushing, shoving and grabbing, one of them was bound to wind up in a cast. Just her luck, she'd be the one held responsible.

Cliff was entirely useless. If anything, he encouraged the mayhem, telling the kids to "go on, get in there" and "don't be a chicken." Ruby wanted to scream at him.

The next instant, she did. "Cliff, keep them away! What if that horse kicks?"

"They're fine."

Fine? Had he lost his mind? Where were the helmets and the protective vest? Behind the chutes, that was where.

Ruby started in that direction, only to be cut off by Erin.

"Oops!" She drew up short, barely avoiding a collision with the seven-year-old.

"Sorry," Erin muttered before jetting off.

She was obviously still suspicious of Ruby. What would the girl think when the truth came out? And it would eventually. She'd probably hate Ruby for lying to them all.

In the end, it mattered little. Ruby was leaving soon. But the idea that Erin would harbor ill feelings toward her saddened Ruby. She liked Cliff's family.

Erin caught up with the other youngsters. Besides her sister, Ellie, there was Sam and Annie's two daughters and a boy named Gus. Ruby had been told he belonged to the housekeeper. He was also indisputably the ringleader.

"Something bothering you?" Cliff asked.

She'd been preoccupied and hadn't heard him come up behind her. "Besides the complete lack of adult supervision?" She threw up her hands. "Cliff, we're supposed to be the responsible ones."

"They're just having some fun."

"You're as bad as them," she snapped, then bit her lip. "Sorry."

"Is it the arraignment?"

The fight went out of her. "I take it you heard."

"Detective James called me earlier. Said it was postponed."

"Thanks to Crowley's attorneys."

"What are you going to do?"

Cliff was asking if she was staying in Sweetheart or going home.

"I haven't decided."

Ellie came bounding over. "Uncle Cliff! Can we start dressing the goats now?"

"Let me handle this." Ruby said, grateful for the interruption.

Outfitting two Nubians in old denim shorts, button-down shirts, bandannas, and cowboy boots on all four hooves was no easy feat. The object of the game was to see which team could dress their goat first.

The Nubians refused to cooperate. Were they not tethered to a stake in the ground, they would have run off. The hardest part of the game was keeping the boots on.

By some miracle, no children or animals were harmed during the practice runs. In the end, the goats and horses received treats and everyone had a good laugh. Especially the grown-ups. Evan squealed and squealed. Finally, his mother let him pet one of the goats. When it nibbled his hair, he started to cry.

"There is no pleasing this young man," she complained good-naturedly.

A juice box distracted him and dried his tears. Maeve distributed more juice boxes to all the kids and, for the next few minutes, peace was restored.

Ruby busied herself with undressing the goats and bagging the clothes. Gus helped her return the goats to their pen and the horses to the corral and then walked with her back to the arena. Ringleader or not, he was a good kid.

"Thanks, pal." She rubbed her hand along his buzz-cut hair, surprising herself at how natural the gesture felt.

"No problem." He disappeared to find his friends.

Catching Cliff watching her, she smiled before turning away—and came face-to-face with Maeve. The other woman was alone, having handed off Evan to his sisters.

"You're good for him."

"Gus?" Ruby asked in surprise.

"Good heavens, no." Maeve laughed brightly. "Cliff."

"I'm not sure about that."

"I am. None of us knows exactly what happened with that woman in Reno. He doesn't talk about it. We do know he hasn't developed a serious interest in anyone since then. Except you."

"We're just dating."

Maeve went on as if she hadn't heard Ruby. "I had my doubts at first. Not that you aren't nice. And the kids adore you. But there was just something." Her voice trailed off. "Lately, however, you're different. I can see the two of you together." Her eyes twinkled. "For a long, long time."

Oh, boy. Now Maeve, as well as Erin, was going to hate her when the truth came out.

"I don't want to rush things with Cliff."

"I wouldn't, either, in your shoes. You've both been hurt. Him by that woman and you by your old boyfriend."

Scarlett had discussed Demitri with Maeve? Funny, she was usually so private. Perhaps Cliff was the one to talk. He and his cousin were close.

"Maeve, I…"

"I've put you on the spot. Don't feel like you have to say anything."

"All right." What a relief.

"Maybe you and Cliff can come over for dinner one night this week."

"Okay." If she hadn't left by then.

Cliff believed Crowley was still a threat. Ruby was less convinced but unwilling to take unnecessary risks.

Part of her wanted to stay in Sweetheart. Spend more time with Cliff and explore their feelings. Get to know his nice cousin who was going out of her way to make Ruby feel accepted. But she also wanted to return to Vegas. She missed her job at the casino and her friends. Her condo, too, though she wondered if she'd ever feel safe there again.

Her temples throbbed. It was all so confusing.

Once the equipment was returned to the tack shed and the trash collected, the children were allowed to resume playing—on the lawn in front of the house, not in the arena. They pulled Cliff's hands, enticing him to enter the fray. He refused and, instead, ambled over to where Ruby waited.

"You ready to call it a day?" he asked.

"Right after I finish feeding."

"I'll wait."

She thought of telling him he didn't have to escort her home, then discarded the notion. It would be a waste of breath.

"Come on, Sarge." She called to the dog without thinking, only to hesitate. He didn't belong to her. "Sorry," she told Cliff. "I've gotten used to him."

"He's more than welcome to go with you."

"I won't be borrowing him much longer."

Did that mean she *had* made a decision? Was she going home?

Cliff must have thought so, for disappointment flashed in his eyes.

Sarge trotted alongside Ruby to the barn. A half hour later, she was just finishing her chores when her phone rang. It was Scarlett.

"You need to call your boss," she said when Ruby answered. "He's been trying your old phone and is mad that the number's disconnected. He called me looking for you."

That made sense. Ruby had listed Scarlett as her emergency contact. "Did Ernesto say what's wrong?"

She mimicked Ernesto's thick accent. "Only that he *must* talk to you. *Immediately.*"

Ruby disconnected from her sister and debated whether or not to locate Cliff. He'd been adamant that only he, Scarlett and Detective James have the number for this new phone. But surely calling work wasn't a problem. Ernesto did know her whereabouts, after all.

"Hey, Ernesto. It's me."

"*Chica,* where have you been?"

It was so good to hear his voice. "I'm still in Sweetheart."

"You must come home. Now!"

"I'm not sure I can." Ruby leaned against the stall door. Sugar Pie nuzzled her elbow. "The arraignment's been postponed till next Wednesday. Detective James thinks I should stay here until then."

"Not soon enough." Ernesto sighed expansively. "But it will have to do, I suppose. I will see you next Thursday then. Eleven a.m. sharp."

Ruby laughed. "What's going on?"

"Mr. Xavier and Ms. Lilly are engaged."

"Really! That's great."

The casino owner and the sitcom star had been dating for almost a year. There had been speculation for weeks that he would pop the question.

Everyone at Century Casino liked the star and supported the match. She had a positive effect on their boss and treated all the employees with kindness and courtesy.

"Mr. Xavier's hosting a party a week from Saturday to celebrate," Ernesto said. "The entire VIP lounge has been reserved for the guests. You will simply die, *chica,* when you see the list." He went on to name several TV and movie celebrities. "Mr. Xavier insists you be there."

"Ernesto…"

"You absolutely must come. This is a very important event, and there is so much to do to prepare."

Ruby could commiserate. Events of this size normally required weeks, if not months, of preparation.

"You owe me, *chica*."

She did owe Ernesto. He'd gone to bat for her, helping her land the job as his assistant when there were other more experienced candidates for the job.

"I'll call you in the morning," she said, wanting to give herself a little time to think about it.

"With good news." Ernesto's tone contained the merest hint of a warning.

"Talk to you then. Goodbye." She flipped the phone shut and shoved it in her pocket.

Here was the chance she'd been waiting for. An excuse to return to Vegas. She hadn't just given Cliff lip service when she claimed her job was in jeopardy.

Securing the stall doors, Ruby left the barn. Cliff was in the driveway, bidding goodbye to his cousin and her children. Their gazes connected. And stayed connected. Her heart fluttered.

By the time she reached Cliff, she was less sure about returning to Vegas than she'd been a minute ago and fairly certain she'd have disappointing news for Ernesto when she called him in the morning.

What was one more week? She'd still make it back in time for the engagement party.

# Chapter Ten

A shrill buzz filled the station seconds before the door swung wide. Cliff strode forward to greet their visitor. Iva Lynn glanced up from her computer, and her jaw went slack.

Detective James stood at least six-five and was built like a freight train. He'd called Cliff earlier to say he wanted to deliver this latest development to Ruby personally. He'd taken a special interest in her case and felt responsible for her safety. Cliff didn't argue. The more people interested in her case, the better for her.

"You made good time." Cliff shook the other man's hand.

"There isn't a minute to lose."

After a brief introduction, he said to Iva Lynn, "I'll call when we know more."

She'd been assigned to remain at the station in case an update on Crowley came in while Cliff and Detective James were at the Gold Nugget.

The two men left in Cliff's SUV. He didn't engage the flashers on the chance Crowley or one of his hired minions was in Sweetheart.

When they were on the road, he called Sam and advised him of their ETA. Cliff had included his friend in the latest developments in order that he keep a watch on Ruby and an eye out for Crowley. After the events of last night, they could no longer count on Crowley's aversion to crowds.

"There's a gymkhana going on today," Cliff informed Detective James.

"A what?"

"Fun and games for the family. Roping, team penning, pony rides, mutton busting."

"Mutton busting?" The young detective's laugh reverberated from deep in his chest. "I'm not going to ask what that is." The next instant, he sobered. "You've gotten close to Ruby these past ten days. How's she going to take the news?"

"Not well. She'll panic."

"I think so, too. We need a backup plan."

"Been working on that."

James sent him a curious look but didn't press for details. "I'll leave it to you."

The ranch was swarming with guests and locals when they arrived. Cliff had to park a good hundred yards from the main house. Nerves, combined with the hotter than normal weather, caused both men to sweat profusely. Passing a makeshift snack bar, they drew stares from everyone.

Cliff could imagine the whispered conversations.

"Who's that man with the sheriff?"

"He's wearing a badge on his belt."

"Must be official business."

"What kind of official business?"

They bypassed the arena and headed straight to the barn. Cliff didn't want Ruby spotting them before they had a chance to talk to her.

"Wait here," Cliff said once he and James were inside. "I'll bring her."

The detective produced a handkerchief and wiped his brow. "What's that smell?"

"Horses."

He lifted a foot and inspected the sole of his shoe. "Am I safe?"

"Watch your step."

"Damned if you country boys don't live a different life."

"Be right back."

Cliff ignored the many familiar faces and friendly hellos. He'd spotted Ruby at the chutes, readying children and ewes for mutton busting, the final event of the day. Sam was with her. Good.

Upon seeing Cliff, she smiled happily. "Hey! Just in time. Ellie's next."

He came up beside her and lowered his mouth to her ear. "We need to talk. Now."

"Cliff, I can't. The sheep—"

"Sam will take over for you."

"Go," Sam said and waved to one of the other wranglers. "I've got this handled."

Her glance traveled from one man to the other. When she spoke, her voice was strained. "What's wrong?"

"Not here." Cliff grabbed her arm and propelled her away from the chutes. "Try to act natural," he whispered.

"You're kidding, of course." They broke free of the crowd, and she demanded, "What exactly's going on?"

"Detective James is here."

Her steps faltered. Cliff tightened his hold on her and continued walking.

It was the first time they'd touched since dinner on Monday. Five days. Cliff wished it was under different circumstances.

"Is Crowley here?" she asked.

"We don't know."

"Don't know!" Her voice rose. "That's your answer?"

"Detective James will fill you in."

"It's bad, isn't it?" Ruby's demeanor changed from oppositional to compliant.

"It's not good."

"How you doing, Ruby?" Detective James asked when they entered the barn.

"That depends. Why are you here?"

"Have a seat." He'd been busy while Cliff was fetching Ruby. An upside-down wooden bucket sat next to a saw-horse. "I insist."

Ruby sat on the bucket with obvious reluctance. Detective James perched on the sawhorse. Cliff was more comfortable standing.

"Has the arraignment been postponed again?" She hugged her middle as if cold.

"No," James said carefully. "The charges against Crowley have been dropped."

"Dropped!" She shot to her feet. "You can't be serious."

"Please sit."

"He attacked me. There were witnesses. DNA evidence." Her hands sliced the air in front of her. "My God, he should be going to trial."

"You're right."

She went toe-to-toe with James, ignoring his considerably larger size. "Crowley is a stalker. A criminal. A monster. And he's getting off. How is it possible?"

"His attorneys uncovered an…oversight, shall we say, in the arrest process."

"An oversight?" Daggers flew from her eyes.

"Procedure wasn't followed appropriately. A step was skipped during booking, the fault of a rookie."

"This is bullshit!" she yelled.

Cliff completely agreed. It wasn't fair that the same laws designed to protect the innocent sometimes allowed the guilty to go free. All he and Detective James could do now was protect Ruby.

"There's more," Detective James said.

Cliff braced himself for Ruby's reaction. It could go either way. Tears or rage.

She sank onto the bucket. "I don't think I can take more."

"Crowley went to the casino last evening looking for you."

She gasped.

"When you weren't there, he accosted your manager, Ernesto Alverez. Roughed him up a little."

"Oh, no!" She began to cry. "Is he all right?"

"Shaken, but otherwise unharmed."

"I hope to God he filed charges against Crowley."

"He did," James said. "But as Mr. Alverez wasn't hurt, the charges are only misdemeanors."

Ruby wiped her nose with her sleeve and expelled a shaky breath.

Cliff moved closer. He'd give anything to hold her in his arms.

"It gets worse," James said.

"How?"

"Ernesto may have mentioned your sister, Scarlett."

"He did!"

"He's not sure." James cleared his throat. "He was pretty rattled, and Crowley's intimidating."

Ruby visibly trembled. "Crowley knows I'm in Sweetheart."

The hell with it, Cliff thought and squeezed her arm. "He doesn't necessarily know. Ernesto thinks he said something like, why don't you ask her sister and leave me alone. He swears he didn't say you were in Sweetheart."

"He might as well have."

"It's going to be all right, Ruby."

She glared up at him. "Will you quit saying that!"

"If Crowley or his men come here, all they're going to find is Scarlett. Not Ruby. You just have to keep playing the part."

Her facade began to crumble. "I'm afraid."

"I know you are, honey." The endearment just slipped out.

Ruby didn't appear to notice. Detective James did, and he studied Cliff long and hard.

Cliff maintained his cool. Perhaps the Vegas police detective had learned about his previous misconduct. Perhaps not. He'd get no confirmation from Cliff.

"I think I should go to my dad's in North Dakota." Her voice was soft and thready.

"You could," James agreed. "But Crowley will look for you there, if he hasn't already. The odds are better if you stay here."

"The guy is crazy," she insisted. "And he's after me. When is this going to stop?"

"I wish I had an answer for you."

"Right." Her agitation increased. "He's going to have to attack me again. And this time, there can't be some rookie screwing up the arrest."

"What you need to do is file a restraining order against him," Cliff said.

"There's already an order of protection in place."

"In Clark County. It wouldn't hurt to have one in Washoe, as well. That way, I can arrest him if he comes near you, and there'll be no loophole for his attorneys to exploit."

"How do I do that?"

"Iva Lynn will help you with the paperwork, and I'll drive you to the courthouse.

James nodded. "That's a good idea."

Having a plan of action seemed to calm Ruby. "What about my job?" She didn't specify which one.

"You may want to take off the next couple of days," Cliff said.

"I thought you told me it would appear suspicious if Scarlett wasn't working."

"It'll be different this time."

"How?" She looked small and vulnerable sitting on the bucket.

Cliff went down on one knee in front of her. "Because you'll be staying with me...24/7."

"In the trailer?"

"My place. I have better locks and a security system."

"Oh."

"You can sleep in the guest room."

She turned to Detective James. "What do you think?"

He shrugged. "Short of hiring a round-the-clock security team, the sheriff is the next best thing."

"It's settled," Cliff rose and gathered Ruby's hand. "We should leave before the gymkhana breaks up."

"What about my things? And Sarge?" Ruby stopped short. "I should let Sam know."

"We'll tell him together. Detective James can wait here."

Cliff felt the other man's eyes boring a hole in the back of his head as he and Ruby exited the barn. He couldn't care less. Let James think whatever he wanted.

Up until three hours ago, Cliff would have claimed his feelings for Ruby were no more than attraction and affection. But when he'd heard about Crowley's altercation with the casino manager, he'd had an instant and powerful urge to protect her with his life and rip Crowley's head off if it came to that.

Not the reaction of someone who was merely fond of another person.

Compelling as they were, however, he had to put his emotions aside. He wasn't about to let any personal involvement hinder his abilities to perform his duty.

Not a second time.

They stopped at the trailer so Ruby could grab a few necessities. She definitely didn't think Cliff was overreacting when he insisted on entering the trailer first, allowing her inside only when the coast was clear. Sarge went with her, watching patiently as she packed her small suitcase.

Ruby took comfort in the dog's normal and unconcerned

behavior. No one had been in the trailer while she was at the ranch.

They didn't stay long and spoke very little on the ride to Cliff's place, her mind racing as she assimilated the events of the past hour.

Crowley was deranged. What other reason could there be for him accosting her boss? Did he think he was untouchable? That the law didn't apply to him?

Poor Ernesto. He was an excellent manager but not exactly a tough guy and probably scared out of his mind. Did he hate her? Hold her responsible? She'd talk to him if she could. *When* she could. After admitting she'd phoned Ernesto the other day, Cliff had nixed contact with him until more was known. More what, she wasn't sure.

Ruby sighed. She might as well forget going home. While she'd recently been considering changes in her life, she'd wanted them to be her choice and on her terms. Not something she was forced into doing out of fear.

"You okay?" Cliff asked.

She sent him a look.

"Okay, dumb question."

Another mile of scenery passed before she said, "I'm sorry about this."

"You have nothing to apologize for."

"I'm inconveniencing you."

He reached across the console for her hand.

She let him hold it. Now wasn't the time to debate right and wrong. She needed comfort.

"All you wanted was to date Scarlett. Not babysit me. And don't tell me it's your duty, blah, blah, blah."

"Okay, I won't. Because it isn't." He took his eyes off the road long enough to send her a penetrating gaze. "I'm doing this, I'm *with* you, because I want to be."

She didn't answer him, letting her thoughts settle around the comment like a warm cloak. Later, when Crowley wasn't a threat, she'd ponder what Cliff had said and the meaning behind it.

His house wasn't what she expected. Then again, she really hadn't known what to expect.

Were she to drive by it, she would have pictured a family with young children living there. Two stories, a peaked tile roof, wide front porch, spacious yard with thick, ankle deep grass, a doghouse, swing set and a basketball hoop affixed above the garage door.

"Very nice," she said, her face pressed to the SUV window.

"Technically, the house belongs to my parents. If I win the election this fall, I'll buy it from them."

"You grew up here?"

"I did." He pressed a button on the sun visor, and the garage door opened.

They pulled in beside a black Mustang convertible. Ruby liked cars and knew a little about them. This one was an older model and beautifully restored.

"I'm impressed," she said as she climbed out of the SUV. "Let me guess, this was yours when you were a teenager."

"Not a teenager." He came around the vehicle and unlocked the house door. "I bought it about ten years ago. A present to myself when I graduated college." He stopped, hand on the doorknob. "One day I'll take you for a ride."

Crowley's unspoken name hung in the air between them. With the charges dropped, one day loomed far into the future.

"I'd like that," Ruby said, surprised at the emotion clogging her throat. She really would like to take a ride with Cliff in his Mustang convertible. "You'd have to put the top down."

"Is there any other way?"

They shared a smile. Ruby was far from relaxed, though she was less stressed. Cliff had that effect on her, made her feel safe and protected. It wasn't just the uniform and the gun and the special training he'd received. He cared about her.

The inside of his home was as comfortable as the outside. Cozy, functional furniture. Colorful throw rugs on the floors. Knickknacks on the shelves.

Sarge made a sweep of the place. Satisfied no danger lurked, he retired to his bed in a nook by the fireplace.

"You hungry?" Cliff asked.

"I can't ask you to feed me, too."

"Don't worry about it. My cousin and aunt are always pawning off leftovers on me. There's a casserole in the fridge and half a loaf of French bread on the counter."

"What can I do to help?"

"Make a salad?" he suggested.

"Point me in the right direction."

Actually, Cliff left her on her own in the kitchen while he took care of some necessities around the house. When he returned twenty minutes later, she'd set the table, had the bread warming in the oven and the casserole heating in the microwave.

"Hope you don't mind," she said, chopping greens on a cutting board. "I sort of made myself at home."

His stare held hers for several heartbeats. "I don't mind at all."

Ruby felt her cheeks flush. "Should be ready in another five minutes."

"You want something to drink?"

He'd changed at some point, from his uniform into cargo shorts and a T-shirt. He looked...great.

"Water's fine." Two simple words, yet her tongue tripped over them.

Cliff mistook the reason. "Crowley has you on edge."

"Yeah, he does." *Him and someone else.*

During dinner Ruby tried to ignore the subtle sparks

passing between them. Cliff didn't appear aware of them. That, or he wasn't bothered. She insisted on washing the dishes when they were done.

"I'll take Sarge outside," he said.

"Do you mind waiting? It's such a nice night. I'm a little nervous about being alone."

"All right."

It was a half-truth. Okay, a quarter truth. She *was* worried Crowley might show up. Mostly she just wanted to prolong her time with Cliff.

Though still warm outside, a mild breeze made their short stroll around the backyard pleasant.

"What an awesome tree house," she exclaimed. "You and your dad build it?"

"We did. I was nine."

"Don't tell me, you fell out of it and broke your arm."

"No, but my dad did."

"You're joking."

He laughed. "In three places."

They were quiet for a bit while Sarge patrolled the entire fence line. Cliff's next question surprised her.

"Why are you and Scarlett so different? Isn't that strange for identical twins?"

"I suppose. It probably started at a young age. Our mom wasn't one of those parents who dresses their children alike. She encouraged our individually. We grew up with different friends and different interests and different styles. More like typical sisters than twins. Then, our parents divorced."

"What happened?"

"Between them? I suppose they grew apart. No indiscretions, no secret gambling problems. They did fight a lot."

"Between you and Scarlett," Cliff clarified.

"Ah."

By silent consent, they sat on the porch swing rather

than return inside. Sarge stood next to Ruby with his head on her leg while she absently stroked his large, furry ears.

"Scarlett took the divorce badly and blamed Dad. Not for the problems he and Mom had but for not staying and working through them."

"And you didn't?"

Ruby and Cliff were sitting close enough that their thighs brushed. Only two layers of material separated them, his shorts and her jeans. The realization sent a jolt of awareness coursing through her. Concentrating became difficult.

"Of course I wanted my parents to stay married. Doesn't every child? But I was old enough to understand they were miserable and making everyone else miserable. Better to end the marriage and maybe find someone else. Scarlett didn't see it that way. She cut Dad out of her life. Fortunately, they reconciled a few years later. Still, things have never been the same with them. Or us."

"She felt betrayed."

"You're right." Ruby swiveled to face him. "That's pretty astute for someone whose parents are still together."

"I watched the same thing happen to my nieces when Maeve and their dad divorced. Erin especially suffered."

"That's a shame." Ruby thought the divorce might explain some of the girl's coolness toward her.

Cliff pushed with his feet to start the swing gently swaying. "Tell me about the men who have gone down in the annals of history as your boyfriends."

She smiled at his use of her earlier phrase. "Not much to tell."

"You've never married?"

"Nope."

"Close?"

"Mmm…a little close. We went together off and on for a couple of years. Probably why I'm so hard on Scarlett and

Demitri. I can't help thinking if it's meant to be, the relationship would be easier. Less drama."

"You're a romantic," Cliff said.

"Me? Hardly. They just have too many obstacles."

"Yeah." He shifted away from her.

Was he thinking of them? They certainly had obstacles facing them. Or of Talia?

She needed to stay focused where Cliff was concerned. Wild attraction aside, they couldn't take their relationship one step further. If only for the reasons she'd just stated.

"We should probably head inside." He scanned the horizon where a fiery sun had begun to dip below the pine-covered mountaintops. "You've had a long day."

It *had* been a long day. And draining. What with the gymkhana and then the visit from Detective James, she should be exhausted. Only she wasn't. Sitting next to Cliff, feeling the warmth of his leg pressed to hers, had energized her.

She stood, not about to give him any insight into what was going through her head. "I could use a shower."

His eyes widened slightly at her remark. The next instant, the look was gone. "There are fresh towels in the hall bath."

Having said she could use a shower, Ruby was left with no choice but to take one. She tried not to think of Cliff thinking of her as she stepped under the warm spray. Staying at his house, *with* him, was an exercise in restraint. She shouldn't have agreed.

But, then, she'd be alone in the trailer and a sitting duck if Crowley showed up.

Wrapped in a terrycloth robe she'd found hanging on a hook behind the door, she emerged from the bathroom, letting residual steam escape into the hall as she did.

A softly uttered, "Wow," stopped her.

Cliff stood not ten feet away, his hand poised above the alarm panel, his gaze riveted on her and hunger flaring in his eyes.

Suddenly self-conscious, Ruby lifted a hand to her damp hair.

He waited, frozen in place, as if daring her to scurry across the hall to the security of the guest room. She took a tentative step…

…toward him.

"Cliff."

He reached her in three long strides. The next instant, she was in his arms, her back arched and his mouth dangerously close. So close, she could taste his breath and hear the beat of his pounding heart.

"There are a hundred reasons we shouldn't do this." He threaded his fingers into her hair and tilted her head to the absolute perfect angle for kissing.

"And a hundred reasons we should," she whispered, closing her eyes as his lips claimed hers.

## Chapter Eleven

Ruby fell backward onto Cliff's king-size bed, pulling him on top of her as she did. Leaning on his elbows, he stared into her face. A light from the hall provided just enough illumination for her to distinguish his features. The trace of doubt reflected there couldn't be denied.

"It's not the same," she said, cradling his cheeks in her palms. "You and I, this is different."

He ground into her, the evidence of his desire a thick ridge pushing against her belly. "I'm not thinking of anyone or anything else but you. I swear."

That wasn't quite true, as the trace of doubt revealed. But the past wouldn't haunt them. Not tonight. She'd make sure their relationship resulted in no crossing of boundaries, no compromising of careers, and she certainly wasn't playing him for information.

"Are you sure?" he asked, his fingertips skimming the curve of her jaw.

If he was giving her one last chance to back out, she wasn't taking it.

"Very sure."

"This isn't a casual fling for me."

"For me, either." She arched into him. "There's been no one since—"

He cut her off with a searing kiss. It was what she'd been hoping for. What she'd craved. He didn't disappoint, breaking the kiss only when she could take no more and begged him to stop.

"On one condition." He grinned wickedly.

"What's that?"

"This." He untied the belt to her robe and parted the thick folds of material. His gaze went straight to her naked breasts and lingered. "You're exquisite."

Desire consumed her. "Touch me."

"I'm going to do more than that."

Cupping her breast, he brought his mouth to the already taut nipple and sucked greedily. She sighed, urging him on. His mouth moved to her other breast, then to the valley between them.

The sensation was incredible. And not nearly enough. Her skin ached to be caressed. Her needs demanded to be met.

"Take these off," she said, the button to his cargo shorts defeating her clumsy fingers.

"Yes, ma'am." He nudged her hand aside.

With the front of his shorts open at last, she yanked his T-shirt free from the waistband.

"Wait," he growled.

"That's asking a lot."

He stood and tore off the T-shirt, throwing it aside. *Nice abs!* Ruby watched with avid interest as he removed his athletic shoes and peeled away his socks. Now came the really interesting part.

She rose to her knees, the robe falling open. Cliff hesitated. Purring seductively, she slid the robe off. It pooled onto the bed behind her.

A ragged moan emanated from deep in his chest. "Ruby, you're…"

"Hurry," she pleaded.

Hooking his thumbs in the sides of his shorts, he shed them and his underwear in one fluid motion.

She stared, unable to move. He was everything, all her

fantasies rolled into one. Tanned skin covered hard muscles. A smattering of hair darkened his chest and trailed in a line down his stomach. Broad shoulders. Narrow hips. All man. All male. All hers.

Scooting to the edge of the bed, she wrapped her arms around his neck. The sensation of her naked breasts against his chest was heaven.

"Kiss me," she said. What she really wanted was for him to toss her onto the bed and ravage her.

"Not yet."

Seriously! She was about to complain when he reached for the nightstand drawer, opened it and removed a condom. Okay. One of them was thinking clearly. He set the small packet aside.

"Aren't you going to…" She motioned with her hand.

That brought a smile to his lips. "Eventually."

Gathering her into his arms, he kissed her. This time, however, there was nothing tender about it. The room momentarily tilted as he pushed her onto the mattress, then faded away as he lay on top of her. There was only him and her and this moment.

He teased her with nimble fingers. Tantalized her with moist kisses. Seduced her with erotic words. Slowly, patiently, he learned her body. What felt good. What felt great.

When one more stoke of his finger or flick of his tongue would have sent her flying over the edge, she stopped him with a harsh, "No, not yet."

"Did I—"

"My turn."

He didn't object when she rolled him onto his back and indulged her every whim. It took a while. She had a lot of whims.

"Enough," he growled when he could endure no more.

She consoled herself with, "There's always next time."

Tearing open the condom, he sheathed himself. "Now, Ruby."

"Now what?" she asked coyly.

He was obviously a subscriber to the philosophy of less talk, more action, for, without any wasted effort, he settled her solidly onto his middle. She leaned down and sought his mouth.

He stopped her before she could satisfy another of her whims. "Say it," he demanded, his intense gaze searching her face.

"I want you," she murmured, rocking her hips back and forth.

"Not that."

What then?

All at once, it came to her. As surely as she knew they were in this for the long haul.

"Make love to me, Cliff."

Drawing in a harsh breath, he grabbed her by the waist and positioned her above him. Ruby guided him inside her, crying out as he entered. Not from pain but pleasure. He plunged deep, thrusting slowly at first, then faster. Their foreplay had been drawn out and so incredibly sensuous, she was ready to climax within seconds.

This time, she couldn't stop. Didn't dare stop. The next instant, it was upon her, wave after wave of delight.

The last tremor had barely begun to fade when Cliff raced to his own shuddering release. She held him tight, moaning his name over and over.

She *might* have said something else. Something revealing about her feelings for him. Oops. Well, too late now. Maybe he hadn't heard.

After a moment, when his breathing slowed, she sat up.

He held her in place with an arm around her waist. "Don't leave."

"I won't go far, I promise."

Was there more to his question and her answer?

With slightly stilted movements, she climbed off him and stretched out beside him. He gathered her to his side.

"I suppose we need to talk about what just happened," he said.

"Yeah."

At least he didn't want to talk about what had accidentally slipped out in the throes of passion. Had she simply imagined it?

"I want to see you again."

"Hard to avoid me. I am staying with you."

"I mean later."

Later as in when she returned to Vegas.

"Okay." More than okay. She was glad. Really glad. "You said before the distance was manageable."

"What if you stayed in Sweetheart?"

She should have been prepared for that. Cliff didn't give his heart lightly. Neither did she, for that matter.

"I have a job."

"Crowley's on the loose."

There was that. "Do you really think he'll come after me?" In the safety of Cliff's arms, secure in his house, she wondered if they hadn't overreacted. "He's not stupid. The police are watching him. And there are the charges Ernesto filed."

"Do you really want to take the chance?"

"It's kind of soon for me to be making big decisions. I realize this sounds stupid since we just made love, but we don't know each other all that well."

"My point. I want to know you better." He brushed a lock of hair from her face, the gesture achingly sweet. "A whole lot better."

"Hard to do that long distance," she mused.

"I'll drive to Vegas on my days off if that's what it takes." The fact that he was willing to go to such lengths impressed her. He *was* in this for the long haul. "If I were to stay, what would I do? Keep working at the Gold Nugget?"

"Unless you don't like it."

"Wrangling isn't the career I've always dreamed of."

"I could talk to my aunt about a job at the Paydirt."

Serving at the local saloon didn't compare to a high-end casino. The pay and tips would be a lot less, too. Not that she'd require as much of an income to live on in Sweetheart as in Vegas.

"What about my condo?"

"Sell it."

That was a step she was nowhere near ready to take. Despite their feelings for each other, things might not work out with Cliff. Look at her sister and Demitri. She could possibly rent the condo to someone at the casino. There were always "apartment wanted" postings in the employee break room.

Refusing to get ahead of herself, Ruby said, "Let me think about it for a day or two. I promised Ernesto I'd come back for the owner's engagement party. I can't disappoint either of them. They've been really good to me." She shrugged one shoulder. "I'll talk to Ernesto when I'm there."

"He's going to try to convince you to stay."

"Probably." Undoubtedly. She snuggled closer to Cliff. "What about Scarlett? She'll come home eventually. If only to get her things. What will we tell people?" Ruby's head started to swim. "How do we explain that you're dating me and not Scarlett?"

"The truth, I suppose."

She made a face. "That's going to sound weird. And maybe a little kinky. Your reputation as the local bachelor will soar."

"You've discovered my secret motive."

She laughed and poked him playfully in the side.

"I don't want to pressure you..." His hand skimmed over the slope of her hip and along her thigh.

"Pressure away." She reached between them, thrilled to find him ready again so soon. "Convince me why I need to stay."

He tensed when her fingers closed around his erection.

It didn't take much. Cliff's negotiating skills were commendable. Within minutes, Ruby was thinking that living in Sweetheart and being with him was exactly what she wanted. Then, she wasn't thinking about anything except how wonderful he felt moving inside her.

An hour later, they abandoned the comfort of his bed in order to let Sarge outside for a final bathroom run. When Ruby's cell phone rang, they both went instantly still.

"Want me to answer it?" Cliff wore only a pair of boxer briefs, yet he managed to look powerful and capable.

She started for the counter where she'd left her purse. "It's probably Scarlett. No one else would call me this late."

Unless it was Detective James with an update on Crowley. A glance at Cliff confirmed he was one step ahead of her.

Ruby glared at the display, a ball of fear lodged in her throat.

"What?" Cliff demanded, coming to her side.

"I don't recognize the number."

He took the phone from her and flipped it open. "Who is this?" Relaxing, he passed the phone to Ruby. "It's your sister."

"Scarlett?" she said. "Where are you calling from?"

"I'm at a convenience store. My battery's dead so the clerk let me use her phone. I take it you and Cliff are together."

"The case against Crowley was dropped. Because of a technicality. I'm staying with Cliff for a day or two in case Crowley comes looking for me." She was intentionally vague.

"Oh, that's bad. I'm sorry." There was a noticeable raw edge to Scarlett's voice.

"Is something wrong?"

Scarlett started to cry. "It's Demitri. We had a fight."

*Another* fight, Ruby thought. "You know how he is. He gets mad and then he's sorry."

"This time is different. We broke up for good. I'm in Blythe now. I'll be home tomorrow morning."

RUBY STARED OUT THE WINDOW, her thoughts scattered and her stomach in knots. Cliff was driving them to the trailer where Scarlett waited. She'd rolled into town an hour ago and had pleaded with Ruby to "come, now." After that, all three of them were heading to the Gold Nugget where they'd let Sam know the sisters' ruse was at an end and Scarlett would be back on the job.

"Nervous?" Cliff asked.

"A little," Ruby confessed.

Funny that he should correctly guess how she felt. Or maybe it wasn't funny. He was astute and observant. He was also learning more about her all the time.

Cliff, it seemed, had taken to heart a fact not many men did. Paying attention to a woman was far more romantic than flowers or candy or candlelit dinners.

"Don't let Scarlett or anyone else pressure you into making a rash decision. Me, included."

Again, he'd guessed correctly. Ruby wasn't so much anxious about the reunion with her sister. Rather, she had the sensation of being pulled in a dozen different directions.

Ernesto wanted her to return to Vegas and the casino. But Crowley was there, possibly waiting for her. The latest from Detective James as of that morning was Crowley had taken refuge in his father's home, evading the reporters and paparazzi stationed outside.

Surely he wouldn't make a move against her. Not when simply leaving the house would be caught on film. Even so, if she were to return to Vegas, she'd spend every second of every day looking over her shoulder and being afraid.

Then, there was Cliff. He wanted her to stay in Sweetheart. With him. He hadn't said as much, but she was quite certain nonetheless.

The path should be obvious, shouldn't it? She was falling for him. Harder each day, as her unintentional admission last night had revealed. Still, she harbored doubts and concerns. Their relationship was brand-new. Untested and untried. Plus, she loved her job in Vegas and hated the idea of leaving it.

A long-distance relationship would certainly be a test.

Damn Crowley. If not for him, Ruby wouldn't be in this position of having to choose.

If not for Crowley, she wouldn't have met Cliff.

"What do *you* want, Ruby?" he asked. "Forget about everyone and everything else."

As if sensing her mood, Sarge whined from the rear seat.

She reached behind her and gave him an absentminded petting. "If I could pick, I'd stay in Sweetheart a little longer. Give us a chance to see where this goes."

"I'd like that." He smiled.

"The only problem is I need gainful employment. One that pays a decent wage and offers some opportunity if possible."

"I wish the town was further down the road to recovery. Things were better before the fire."

"I get that the cost of living is less than Vegas. And I don't always want to be working my tail off. I look at your cousin Maeve and think that maybe I could be like her one day."

"Three kids?"

"Balancing work and my personal life."

"She's good at that."

"And at raising a family."

"Really?" He pretended to clean out his ear. "Did you just say what I think you did? You want kids?"

She laughed. "Maybe not three. One. Or two."

Cliff's house came to mind, ready-made for the next generation of Dempseys. Was she ready for that? Not quite. More like entertaining the possibilities. Weird, until she came to Sweetheart, getting married and having a family was something she considered to be very far into the future.

Two weeks with Cliff had given her an entirely different perspective.

"You'd be a good mom," he said.

"Who'd have guessed?"

"Would you live with Scarlett? If you decide to stay, that is."

"The trailer's pretty small."

"I have plenty of room."

She'd been right. Cliff did want her cohabitating with him.

"How 'bout we take things one step at a time?" She smiled, hoping he understood. "First, I need a job."

"With people coming to town for the Mega Weekend of Weddings, Sam might want to keep both you and your sister on."

"Truthfully, I'd rather work in the hospitality business."

"The offer to talk to my aunt still stands."

Ruby was struck with an idea. The more she rolled it around in her head, the more it appealed to her. "If you don't mind, I'd like to be the one to talk to your aunt. After we tell her about me and Scarlett, of course."

"Sure."

"There's going to be a lot of receptions during the weekend, of weddings, right?"

"I'd say so."

"Your aunt might need a beverage manager. Someone to oversee the drink service for large gatherings."

"She just might." Cliff's nod reflected his approval.

"It would only be temporary," Ruby said.

"Who knows? The whole purpose of the weekend is to put Sweetheart back on the map. Last my aunt said, registration was still climbing. There's another TV crew due in today."

In the meantime, it's possible she could work at the Paydirt as a server. It wouldn't be awful. Might even be enjoyable.

"You should check out the bulletin boards at the community center and the general store." Cliff slowed as they passed a trio of backpackers.

"For jobs?"

"And a place to stay."

"Okay."

No pressure. He was keeping his word.

Ruby let herself relax. It felt good having a plan. One of her own choosing, even if it was tentative.

She'd have to give Ernesto her notice when she returned for the engagement party. He would have a fit. Well, no avoiding that. What if she offered to come back for a long weekend or two? Help train her replacement. Cliff could come with her. For fun, not just protection. Vegas did have a lot to offer by way of excitement.

The good feeling increased—and grew stronger when they came within sight of the trailer. Scarlett's Jeep was parked in front. Until that second, Ruby didn't realize how much she'd missed her twin.

Scarlett must have heard them pull up for she was out the trailer door before Cliff shut off the engine.

Ruby scrambled out of the SUV. Scarlett met her halfway, and they hugged fiercely.

"How are you, honey?" Ruby asked.

Scarlett promptly burst into tears. Ruby should have been prepared. Flashing Cliff an apologetic smile, she walked her sister up the porch steps and into the trailer. They sat on the couch and for twenty minutes, Ruby listened to Scarlett's latest tale of woe.

"It's for good this time," Scarlett said through her tears. "I'm never seeing him again."

Ruby took the teary proclamation in stride. They'd had this same conversation before. Twice before. "I'm sorry he hurt you."

A short time later, Cliff knocked on the door. "Hey, you two."

"Come on in." Scarlett wiped her eyes self-consciously and stood. "Didn't mean to keep you waiting so long."

"No problem."

Sarge hurled past Cliff and charged inside. He went straight for Ruby, who still sat on the couch. Despite his large size, he attempted to crawl onto her lap.

"Sarge, get down!" Scarlett wagged a finger at him, distaste on her face. "You're not supposed to be inside, much less on the furniture."

"My fault," Ruby said, pushing the dog down. "He's been staying with me."

Sarge refused to be parted from her.

"It's my fault, actually." Cliff came over, took Sarge by the collar and coaxed him toward the door. "I insisted Sarge stay with Ruby. For her protection. Guess he's formed some bad habits."

"It's all right." Scarlett sidled closer to Cliff. "I understand."

"I'll put him outside."

"You don't have to." She touched his arm.

Ruby gawked in amazement. Wasn't her sister crying like a baby not five minutes ago?

"Can I get you something?" Scarlett asked, already starting for the kitchen. "A glass of water? It's hot outside."

"Ah, sure."

"How have you been?" She chatted as she fixed Cliff a glass of ice water. "Anything exciting happen while I was gone?" She delivered the water to Cliff, her fingers brushing his during the exchange.

What the heck was going on? Was Scarlett flirting with Cliff. Ruby fumed. She *was* flirting.

Wait a minute! Did her sister think she could pick up with Cliff where she'd left off?

That decided it. Ruby was staying in Sweetheart.

As it turned out, she needn't have worried.

"Well, one thing interesting did happen," Cliff said.

"What's that?" Scarlett smiled winningly.

"Your sister and I are dating."

"You are?" She blinked, pivoting around slowly. Her gaze landed squarely on Ruby. "I see."

"I know you're happy for us," he added.

"I'm...thrilled."

She wasn't, but Ruby didn't care. She rose from the couch, joy cascading through her. Cliff had made his intentions crystal clear.

If her sister weren't watching, she'd go over and kiss Cliff senseless.

*Wait!* Who cared about Scarlett? Certainly not Ruby.

Three seconds later, she was in his arm, Sarge dancing in circles and yipping excitedly.

# Chapter Twelve

Cliff tried not to stare. Now that the two sisters were side by side, the differences were as apparent as a thick black line.

After the announcement that he and Ruby were dating and the kiss she'd given him—his nerve endings were still tingling—Scarlett had wished them well. Whew! For a minute there he'd thought she was hinting at getting back together with him.

The glass of water he'd drank had hit the spot. What he could really use was a second cup of coffee. He had a long day ahead of him and he'd had little sleep the previous night. Ruby, too.

Cliff hoped she stayed in Sweetheart. She'd twice mentioned this morning that their relationship was only in the beginning stages, but he was confident his bachelor days were nearing an end.

"You ready, sis?" Ruby made a pass through the living room, collecting discarded tissues and their empty cups. When she took Cliff's, she smiled at him. His heart kick-started like an infatuated teenager's.

"Yeah, I guess," Scarlett said. She remained seated on the couch.

"What's wrong?"

She expelled a long-drawn-out sigh. "I'm not looking forward to talking with Sam."

"Why?" Ruby expressed sisterly concern.

"He won't be happy with me. With us. We put him through a lot of trouble."

"Sam seems like a decent guy to me." Having set the glasses in the sink, Ruby wiped her hands on a kitchen towel. "He'll be glad you're back on the job."

Personally, Cliff thought his buddy would do well with either sister. Ruby had performed competently, considering her lack of training. His aunt would acquire a good employee if she hired Ruby.

"What about Will?" Scarlett asked. "You said he was onto you. Do we have to tell him?"

"He's going to figure it out as soon as he sees the two of us together." Ruby sat beside her sister on the couch and put a hand on her knee. "It'll be all right."

Ruby may not see it, but Scarlett was stalling. For whatever reason, she didn't want to face the people at the ranch.

He supposed she could be upset from her breakup with Demitri. Or, she was just being Scarlett. The ten-minute-younger, needier twin who counted on her sister to bail her out of trouble and clean up her messes.

Cliff reminded himself that Scarlett had come to Ruby's aid when she need to lie low for a while. Even if it did serve her own purposes at the time. For that reason, he decided to cut her some slack.

They were almost out the door when his phone chimed. The ring belonged to his cousin Maeve. He was instantly on the alert. She didn't call this early on a Sunday unless something was wrong.

"Hey, Maeve."

"Glad I caught you."

"What's up?"

"I know you're probably on duty." She hesitated. "And I hate to impose—"

"Just tell me."

"There's an emergency at the store. The overhead sprinklers sprang a leak. Water's pouring all over the merchandise and flooding the floors. The cleaning crew discovered it when they arrived. Uncle Milt and Mom can't go. They're meeting with the TV crew from Vegas at noon."

The show aired weekdays. The crew was filming for tomorrow's episode.

"I'll meet the repairmen," Cliff said.

"No. I have to go. They need the key to the roof access door, which only I have. Besides, Mom insists."

"Let me guess. You want me to watch the kids."

Her voice grew small. "They only just finished breakfast and aren't dressed yet."

During the summer and on weekends, Maeve let her children sleep in so she could get things done around the house before dropping them off at the sitter's.

"I'm on my way to the Gold Nugget. I could take them along after they're dressed."

"That would be great! I'm probably going to be a while. I hear the place is a mess."

Cliff and his cousin ironed out a few of the details. When he hung up, he explained the situation to Ruby and Scarlett.

"I'll watch them," Scarlett blurted out eagerly. "You and Ruby can go to the ranch."

"It's okay. They love the ranch." He wasn't about to let her off the hook.

"They'll be in the way when you talk to Sam. And I miss them." Scarlett was suddenly on the move when a moment ago she'd sat like a lump on a log. "You said yourself they weren't dressed yet."

Cliff wavered. His gut told him no, to stick with Plan A. Scarlett was shirking her responsibility. Sam had done her a favor every bit as much as he had Ruby, and he deserved an in-person thank-you.

"I think you should come with us." Ruby said, though she didn't insist.

"I'll drop by later with the kids. After I get them dressed."

In other words, after Cliff and Ruby had broken the news to Sam. Did Ruby see how much her sister took advantage of her? Probably not.

He kept his mouth shut. This was none of his business. The sisters' relationship was theirs to deal with. He wouldn't intrude or interfere in any way. "It's up to you," he told Ruby.

"I don't know." She shook her head. "What about Maeve? She may not like the idea."

"Call her." Scarlett suggested, all smiles now.

Maeve was okay with it. Frankly, she sounded so harried, she'd probably have agreed to let old man Seymour watch her brood.

"Hurry," Maeve said and hung up.

Cliff turned to Scarlett. "Come directly to the ranch. No side trips."

"I promise." She held up three fingers in a Boy Scout pledge.

Ten minutes later, they dropped her off at Maeve's. She disappeared through the front door, hauled inside by Erin and Ellie. Good thing Maeve hadn't come out to greet them. She would have noticed Ruby sitting in the front passenger seat.

The conversation with Sam went well. He was also busy. The ranch was hosting a church retreat, turning what was normally a lazy Sunday into a frantic Sunday.

"We're booked solid now through the Mega Weekend of Weddings next month. I could use another wrangler."

"I really appreciate the offer." Ruby smiled up at Sam.

"That sounds like a no."

"I have a couple leads I'd like to explore. In the hospitality field."

"Well, if they don't pan out, give me a call. I happen to be in the hospitality field, too."

"Thank you, Sam." She stood on tiptoes and gave him a peck on the cheek.

"Whoa there!"

If Cliff didn't know better, he'd think his friend was blushing.

"What next?" Ruby asked when she and Cliff were back in the SUV.

"Find you a place to stay? Then check with my aunt. She should be done filming the TV interview by then."

They turned in the direction of town, the community center their intended stop. As they neared the main intersection, they spotted a commotion. A small crowd had gathered and was growing larger by the second.

Ruby craned her neck to see out the windshield. "What's going on?"

Sarge whined and began pacing back and forth in the rear seat.

"The Nevada at Noon TV crew, most likely." Cliff had no sooner spoken than he realized his mistake.

The crowd was visibly agitated, their frantic actions not those of people watching their mayor give an interview. Ruby noticed, too.

"Isn't that the girls and Evan with your aunt?" She turned panicked eyes on Cliff. "Where's Scarlett?"

He swung the SUV into the first available spot. His cell phone rang as he wrenched open the door. It was Iva Lynn.

"Report," he demanded.

"Six people called in. An unidentified man was seen abducting Scarlett McPhee. He was driving a white Infiniti coup. He bore down on her and the children as they were standing outside the general store. According to witnesses, as Scarlett was shielding the children, the man jumped from the car, grabbed her, then wrestled her into the car."

Crowley! It must be him. He'd come for Ruby, only he'd taken Scarlett instead.

Cliff hit the ground running. He could see the children but not if they were all right. "Call Detective Darell James. And the Washoe County Sheriff's office. We're going to need reinforcements."

"Right away."

"The children?" he pushed past people in a frenzy to reach his family.

"They're fine. Scared but unharmed."

Cliff's knees went weak, but he kept moving. "Did anyone get a license plate number or see which direction he went?"

"Both. He took the north road out of town. I'm running the plate now."

He swore under his breath.

"Cliff?" It was Ruby. She'd been running alongside him. "What's happening?" Terror marred her face.

Oh, God. How to tell her that Crowley, the man she feared the most, had taken her sister hostage?

Iva Lynn's voice filled his ear. "Cliff, be careful. Witnesses also reported Crowley has a gun."

"Stay put," Cliff told Ruby in no uncertain terms. "Don't move from this spot for any reason. And keep Sarge with you." He thrust the dog's leash into her hands.

"Okay."

Déjà vu. He'd instructed Scarlett not to make any sidetrips, to go directly to the ranch, only she hadn't.

"I mean it, Ruby." They stood in front of the Perfect Fit Tuxedo shop. Away from all the commotion and prying eyes. Her presence would raise questions, and he had no time to waste explaining.

"I said okay," she snapped.

She was scared. He got that. Not angry at him.

Walking across the street and through the crowd, he found his aunt and cousin waiting with the kids in front of the general store. The site of Scarlett's abduction.

Questioning witnesses wasn't easy. Emotions frequently ran high. Questioning your own family was harder. And children...

Cliff would give anything not to have his nieces and nephew involved.

"Hey, girls."

They turned in unison. "Uncle Cliff!"

He pulled them close and buried his face in their hair, something he hadn't been able to do when he'd first arrived on scene. Thank God they were safe.

"The man took Scarlett," Ellie said, her voice quaking. "You have to get her back."

"I will. I promise."

Evan was in his mother's arms and howling up a storm. That meant he was fine, right? Scared and confused but not hurt.

Scarlett wasn't fine. Crowley had her, and he might not let her go.

What had he been thinking? Cliff mentally kicked himself. He should have seen this coming. Never let Ruby *or* Scarlett out of his sight for one second.

"Shouldn't you be doing something?" His aunt screeched at him.

Speaking of emotions running high.

"I am. I'm interviewing the witnesses." Cliff went down on one knee, putting himself on the same level as his nieces. "I know you're afraid, but I have to ask you some questions. So that I can save Scarlett."

"What kind of questions?" Maeve moved closer. Cliff may be her cousin but she was still hardwired to protect her children.

"Can you tell me what the man looked like?" he asked.

"He was mean," Ellie said. "He said bad words. And he hurt Scarlett. She yelled."

"That's not what Uncle Cliff wants to know," Erin interjected with older sister authority. "He asked what the man looked like."

It was only then that Cliff noticed the well-dressed TV reporter and scruffy camera operator to his left. Shit! They were less than three feet away. Apparently a potential abduction in broad daylight was far more interesting than a chitchat with the mayor about weddings.

"Back off," Cliff barked.

"Can we have an interview, Sheriff?" the reporter asked.

"I said, back off." How long until more reporters arrived?

His expression must have matched his mood, for the reporter and camera operator retreated.

Great. How many other people had witnessed his outburst?

Cliff couldn't worry about that. He had far more important concerns.

"It's okay, Ellie." He reached out and smoothed the younger girl's hair. "Anything you tell me will help us find Scarlett."

"He had black hair." Erin, the bearer of more useable information, stood straighter. "And a mustache. He wore a brown shirt."

Black hair and mustache. The description, though generic, matched Crowley.

"Did you see which way the car went?"

Erin pointed up the road.

"Good job." His niece would make a fine police detective one day.

"What now?" his aunt asked.

"The Vegas police and Washoe County Sheriff's Department are on the way."

"What about Scarlett?"

"We have no idea where he's taken her. Iva Lynn called in an APB. The authorities will be looking for his car."

Much as he hated it and until he had help, questioning

witnesses and gathering information was the best use of his time and resources. The tiniest piece of information might prove invaluable.

Cliff tore himself away from his family and entered the crowd. Additional interviews confirmed Erin's description of Crowley and the events as they'd happened. Scarlett was abducted by a young man driving a white Infiniti. The car had left town by the north road.

He dialed Iva Lynn at the station. She let him know that, in addition to Detective James and the Washoe Sheriff's Department, officers from Carson City were en route.

"Crowley took the north road. Call in for an air support." A helicopter could cover more area in less time than an entire fleet of vehicles.

He no sooner got off the phone than a couple approached him. They'd been returning from a bike ride and stopped when they saw Cliff. Not realizing there was a connection, they had thought to complain about a speeding car that nearly forced them off the road when it made a sharp turn.

"Where was this?"

"About a half mile outside of town," the man said.

The wife glanced at him for confirmation. "I think the sign said Windfall Claim Two Miles."

The old abandoned mine! Was it coincidence or calculated? Had Crowley planned to take Ruby there all along or had he seen the sign and made a spontaneous decision?

Cliff didn't have time to consider an answer. The next instant, Iva Lynn called again.

"Washoe deputies will be here in five."

"Thanks."

He filled Iva Lynn in on Crowley's possible location and that he may be holding Scarlett hostage in the mine. "Put in a call for a hostage negotiator, just in case."

Ignoring the questions being thrown at him from all sides

by concerned citizens and curiosity seekers, he returned to his family.

"What's happening?" His aunt blocked his path. She could be a force when she chose, a skill that served her well as mayor and a business owner.

"Crowley may have taken Scarlett to the Windfall Claim."

"Oh, my God." His aunt covered her mouth with her hands. "Why her? It seems like he targeted Scarlett. That's what people are saying. Is the town in danger?"

She wouldn't let him go without an answer. "He most likely thought Scarlett was Ruby McPhee. Her sister."

"I don't understand." His aunt shook her head. "That makes no sense."

"Scarlett's identical twin sister, Ruby. A man named Crowley, has been stalking her for months. In Vegas. We're assuming he's the one who abducted Scarlett. The description matches."

"Why did he come to Sweetheart?"

"Ruby's here. Has been for the past two weeks. She was hiding from him until his arraignment was over. Except yesterday the charges against him were dropped."

He gave a brief accounting of Ruby's case and how she'd replaced Scarlett at the ranch. Midway through, Maeve joined them, listening intently. The children had been left in the care of Mrs. Yeung, owner of the Sweetheart Wedding Chapel.

Cliff glanced across the street at the tuxedo shop. Good, Ruby hadn't left.

"I don't believe it!" Maeve exclaimed when he was done. "For the past two weeks, the person we thought was Scarlett was really her sister, Ruby?"

The wail of sirens sounded in the distance. The sheriff's department was close. "I've got to go," Cliff said.

Maeve cut him off. She could be as forceful as her mother.

"You let Scarlett watch my children knowing full well that this Crowley character might show up at any minute."

"I'm sorry, Maeve."

"What were you thinking?"

A pair of tourists stood nearby, the man recording the exchange with his phone. Anger surged inside Cliff. He barely refrained from charging over there and plowing his fist into the device. Instead, he drew a breath and faced his cousin.

"You have every right to be angry at me. And we'll deal with this later. But right now, I have a potential hostage situation. Get the kids home right now and let me do my job."

Two official vehicles from the Washoe County Sheriff's Department roared into town and braked to a tire-squealing stop near Cliff's SUV. Right behind them was Iva Lynn's truck. The situation was in immediate need of crowd control.

Cliff assigned Iva Lynn the task, then went and met with Sheriff Eberhardt and his two deputies. Cliff was informed that a third deputy had set up a road block on the south end of town. Another deputy was immediately dispatched to set up a road block on the north side. Who knew what trick Crowley might pull?

While Cliff and Sheriff Eberhardt studied a map of the area and discussed strategy, Detective James called and apprised Cliff of his ETA. Another hour. Well behind the Carson City police who were fifteen minutes out.

From the corner of his eye, Cliff saw his cousin herd her children into the I Do Café. He'd rather she go home as he'd instructed and considered ordering her to do so. His aunt was another matter. She and his uncle stayed. Between them, the crowd, the reporters and every tourist with a phone and a morbid sense of fascination, Cliff felt like a ticking time bomb.

As if he hadn't done that already.

There would be retribution for his mistake. He owed

his family more than an apology. Later. After they rescued Scarlett and Crowley was apprehended.

Iva Lynn skirted the barricade she'd erected with yellow crime-scene tape. "The hostage negotiator will be here within an hour. He's supposed to be one of the best around."

"Call me when he arrives."

"Are you heading to the mine site?"

"After I stop at the station." He didn't have to tell Iva Lynn why. They both knew he was after weapons and ammunition. "I'm depending on you to hold down the fort."

"Count on it, Sheriff."

"Cliff?"

At the sound of Ruby's teary voice, he pivoted, and his heart tripped.

"I told you to wait at the shop."

"Please." She absentmindedly threaded Sarge's leash through her fingers. "I'm worried about Scarlett. What's going on?"

"It's possible Crowley's taken her to the Windfall Claim."

Her eyes widened. "Why there?

A confined space in which to control his hostage. A high vantage point to see what was coming.

"We're going to get her back, honey."

"I want to go with you."

"Not a chance. Iva Lynn!" he hollered. The older woman hurried over. "Do not let Ruby go anywhere that isn't indoors and out of sight."

"I'll keep a watch on her."

The next instant, the very situation Cliff had hoped to avoid occurred. Maeve and the kids charged out of the café, donuts in the girls' hands.

Ellie spied Ruby and promptly ran toward her. "It's Scarlett. You're okay."

Maeve chased after her, Evan bouncing on her hip and

dragging Erin along with her free hand. "Ellie, get back here."

The girl skidded to a stop a few feet in front of Ruby, her mother and sister bumping into her like a trio of bumbling Keystone Kops. "You're not Scarlett," Ellie said.

Cliff saw panic flare in Ruby's eyes. Evidently his cousin hadn't told her children the full story. "It's her twin sister, Ruby," he said.

"Sister?" Erin frowned.

Ellie, on the other hand, beamed. "That's cool."

"Dempsey!" the sheriff from Washoe beckoned him while simultaneously speaking into the radio attached to his uniform. "We need to leave now!"

Crowley must have been spotted!

Ruby held his arm, restraining him. "Please be careful. And bring my sister home."

"I'll call Iva Lynn with any updates."

She threw her arms around his neck. Though he couldn't spare another second, he hugged her back. Grabbing Sarge's leash, he sped off, the dog trotting beside him.

Engaging his flashers and siren, he followed the Washoe sheriff out of town and to the Windfall Claim. From the backseat, Sarge barked.

Cliff reached behind him to ruffle the dog's fur. "Ready to go to work, buddy?"

"THIS IS ALL YOUR FAULT!"

Ruby spun, shocked to find Mayor Dempsey literally in her face. "I'm s-sorry."

"My grandchildren could have been injured. Or worse." She choked on the last word. "Did that ever occur to you?"

Ruby was grateful Cliff's cousin had decided to leave and take the kids with her. She didn't want more people than had already gathered to witness the mayor's outburst.

She was also grateful for Iva Lynn's proximity. After

Cliff's stern dictate, the deputy wasn't letting Ruby out of her sight, angry mayor or no angry mayor. That was fine with her. She didn't want to miss one update regarding her sister.

"Cliff told Scarlett not to go anywhere except the Gold Nugget," Ruby said. "I don't know what she was doing here."

The mayor talked over Ruby, would have stomped over Ruby if she could get away with it. "You should never have come to Sweetheart. We've got enough problems as it is."

No point trying to explain Ruby and Scarlett's original plan. Or that Scarlett had thrown a wrench in it by returning early.

Was it possible? Had that been what tipped Crowley off? He must have had Demitri watched, too.

How could Ruby and Cliff have been so stupid?

But wouldn't Crowley have known he was grabbing Scarlett and not Ruby? Did he even care which sister he had?

Her throat burned with unshed tears and unexpressed frustration. She would never forgive herself for this.

"I'm sorry," she repeated to the mayor and covered her face with her hands.

"If even one person is harmed or suffers because of this, you will be a lot more than sorry, young lady."

Hard to imagine this was the same woman Ruby had considered petitioning for a job a mere hour ago.

Like she cared now. If anything happened to Scarlett...

Mayor Dempsey jabbed the air with her finger. "I'll have you arrested for endangerment—"

"That's enough!" Iva Lynn planted herself between the mayor and Ruby. "Leave her alone."

The mayor drew herself up. "Need I remind you who you work for?"

"Need *I* remind *you* who's in charge of this situation?"

"She brought danger to us."

"Stop it!" Ruby yelled. "Stop it now!" She wheeled on

the mayor. "Your grandchildren are safe. Nothing happened to them other than a scare. A bad one but still just a scare."

A sob broke free. "My sister's in the hands of a lunatic."

The mayor instantly sobered. "Of course, we all hope she's safe. I didn't mean…"

Ruby broke into uncontrolled tears.

An arm went around her shoulders. It belonged to Iva Lynn. When she spoke, it was in a low voice and directed at the mayor.

"There's a reporter right there and the camera is rolling. Unless you want the rest of this 'oh, so nice' scene played out on national television, I suggest you shut up."

The mayor blanched.

"Come on, now," Iva Lynn said to Ruby. "Let's go to the café. A cup of coffee will do you good."

She didn't want any coffee. All she wanted was her sister back and for this nightmare to end.

It wasn't going to happen anytime soon. She and Iva Lynn had just taken seats at the café counter when the deputy's phone rang.

"Yes, Sheriff." Iva Lynn remained stoic during the entire brief conversation. "I'll tell her. Good luck." A pause followed. "No, neither one of them is here yet…Right. Will do."

"Tell me what?" Ruby demanded the instant Iva Lynn hung up.

The other woman took hold of her hand and squeezed it hard. "Cliff, Sheriff Eberhardt and the two deputies have made it to a ravine at the base of the mine. They spotted Crowley at the entrance."

"Oh, my God!" Ruby's vision dimmed as the strength drained from her.

"Ruby, listen to me." The pressure from Iva Lynn's hand increased. "Scarlett was also spotted. Crowley has her, but she's alive. You hear me? She's alive."

For the moment. Ruby knew better than anyone the violence Crowley was capable of committing and the sick way his mind worked.

# Chapter Thirteen

The team had taken position approximately fifty yards from the mine. Cliff peered through a pair of binoculars. No change from the last time he checked three minutes ago.

Crowley and Scarlett were just inside the mine entrance. Both moving and apparently talking, though what they said didn't carry down the hill to where Cliff, Detective James, two Carson City P.D. officers, Sheriff Eberhardt, his deputies and the hostage negotiator crouched in the brush or behind trees.

On the hill to their left, a SWAT sniper and spotter kept Crowley in their sights. Per orders, the sniper's assault rifle was loaded with rubber bullets. They would not risk Scarlett becoming collateral damage.

The good news: she was alive and, for now at least, unharmed. The bad news: Crowley held her captive.

Tensions ran high among the team. This was a waiting game. Cliff despised feeling helpless, but, after countless stakeouts during his years with Reno Drug Investigations, he knew the value of maintaining a cool head. The slightest thing could set Crowley off, and the results were guaranteed to be disastrous.

They'd seen his pistol when he'd waved it around, proclaiming to one and all he was armed. Yes, he'd spotted them. He may not know exactly how many of them there were or about the sniper, but he was no fool.

He was also strung out on drugs. Cocaine or crack was Cliff's guess. The telltale signs were easy to spot. Erratic behavior. Restlessness. Paranoia.

Sarge nudged Cliff's hand, offering his silent support. "I know, boy. I don't like it, either."

"Bring me Ruby! Now. You hear me?" Crowley's shout carried loud and clear down the hill.

Everyone on the team instantly froze.

"You got thirty minutes." Crowley emerged from the mine entrance. "If Ruby's not here by then, something's going to happen to her pretty sister. And I guarantee you won't like it."

Cliff raised the binoculars to his eyes, bringing Crowley into focus.

The sheriff's radio crackled to life. "I have a shot," the SWAT sniper said.

"No!" Cliff shouted.

At the same moment, the sheriff ordered, "Hold your fire. The woman's in the way."

Crowley had pushed Scarlett out in front of him, his hand gripping her arm like a steel vise. Her clothes were torn, her face dirty and her hair disheveled. Otherwise, she appeared unharmed.

"He finally figured out he has the wrong sister." Detective James's statement was issued matter-of-factly. There was nothing matter-of-fact about his hunkered-down stance. He looked like a bull ready to charge.

"She probably told him. I would in her shoes."

Cliff would try anything to secure her freedom. Perhaps Scarlett thought Crowley would release her once he learned of his mistake.

Instead he was using Scarlett to get what he really wanted. Ruby.

"Thirty minutes," Crowley repeated. Then he did something everyone had hoped he wouldn't. He shoved Scarlett to her knees and put the barrel of the pistol to her head. "Or she dies."

Detective James swore ripely.

The hostage negotiator raised the bullhorn to his mouth. He was a middle-aged man with glasses. Hardly the type one would take for a trained crisis-situation interventionist. Of the entire team, he remained the most calm and collected. Then again, he had to.

"Look, Crowley," he said, his tone friendly and helpful. "You don't want to hurt her. It will only make things worse for you. Murder on top of kidnapping. You'll spend the rest of your life in prison. Think of your family."

"I want Ruby!" Crowley wrenched Scarlett's arm.

She let out a cry.

"Shut up!" He pushed her head down, then pressed the pistol to the back of her neck. "Better hurry."

Cliff tried not to react. Instead he studied the area immediately surrounding the mine entrance.

"Crowley, listen to me," the negotiator said. "Your father will be here soon."

The senior Crowley had been contacted the moment it was confirmed his son had Scarlett. Cliff wasn't sure what they thought the man could do. His relationship with his son wasn't the stuff of Hallmark greeting-card commercials and could well push Crowley over the edge.

That wasn't a chance Cliff was willing to take.

"My father?" Crowley screamed and waved his gun in the air. "I don't want that son of a bitch anywhere near me!"

Scarlett had curled into a ball on the ground at Crowley's feet, as if by making herself small he wouldn't notice her. He did and kicked her, causing her to cry out again.

Cliff's blood heated to a rapid boil. His hand inched toward his own gun.

"Stay cool, man."

Cliff wasn't sure if Detective James was talking to him or to Crowley. Maybe to both of them.

"I have a clean shot." The sniper's voice exploded from the radio.

This could be their last chance. Still, Cliff didn't like the odds. Crowley had proven his unpredictability and propensity to violence. If they missed or failed to incapacitate him, he could take his rage out on Scarlett.

Tear gas might be a better option. Getting close enough to deliver it without Crowley picking them off was the problem.

He turned to James. "What do you think? He's your perp."

The detective didn't hesitate. "Take the shot."

"Fire." Sheriff Eberhardt commanded.

At the same instant, Crowley bent down to grab Scarlett. The bullet split the air where he'd been standing an instant earlier. Crowley hit the ground near Scarlett. She screamed and covered her ears. The next two shots missed Crowley by inches.

He was too close to Scarlett!

"Cease-fire," Eberhardt hollered into his radio. "Repeat, cease-fire."

Damn, it couldn't have gone more wrong.

Crawling on all fours, Crowley dragged Scarlett back inside the mine. Once there, he yelled down to them. "Bring Ruby to me now or her sister's a dead woman.

One of the CCPD officers answered his ringing phone. "Crowley's father is twenty minutes out."

The negotiator wiped the sweat from his forehead. "I suggest we wait for him."

"I have a better idea." Cliff straightened.

"No heroics," Sheriff Eberhardt warned.

Cliff nodded at the negotiator. "You keep him distracted. Lure him out of the mine. Lie to him. Tell him that Ruby's on her way and wants to see her sister first before the exchange is made."

The sheriff looked displeased. "What are you planning, Dempsey?"

"Just be ready. And watch for my signal." Cliff started forward through the brush, Sarge following him.

"Come back here." The sheriff's order was delivered through gritted teeth. He wouldn't shout. Crowley might hear.

Cliff kept going. He didn't need binoculars or a map. He'd come to the Windfall Claim countless times as a boy with his father and then as a teenager with friends.

The shaft opening was five feet tall at the center. Four feet wide. It was built into the side of a hill thick with ponderosa pines and scrub oaks. Most importantly, a rocky ledge jutted out from the top.

It wasn't large. Just the right size to hold a man and a dog.

The footpath leading up the back side of the mine had deteriorated in the decade since Cliff last climbed it, making the going rough. Even with only three legs, Sarge managed better than him and was waiting at the top when Cliff got there.

He was tempted to fire off a smart retort but didn't. Too close. Crowley might hear.

Inch by inch, Cliff crawled to the ledge, making as little noise as possible. From his vantage point, he couldn't see the mine entrance beneath him. No need. Crowley was in there.

Sarge knew it, too. Nostrils quivering, the dog stretched his nose out to catch the scent. When he emitted a soft whine, Cliff laid a hand on his back, quieting him.

Down in the ravine, the hostage negotiator attempted to engage Crowley in dialog. Half of Crowley's responses made no sense, his grip on reality slipping. Once, he called Scarlett by the name of an earlier alleged victim. Another time, by his brother's name.

Cliff continued moving closer to the edge. When he was in prime position, slowly, very slowly, he raised his arm in the air.

"Crowley," the hostage negotiator's voice rang out. "I just got a call. Ruby's on her way. She'll be here any minute."

The team had seen Cliff's signal and knew he was ready.

"She won't agree to the exchange without first making sure her sister's okay. You need to bring Scarlett out."

"And have you take another shot at me?" Crowley roared. "Like hell."

Cliff lay utterly still, listening. He had to admit the negotiator was good. Using Crowley's own words against him and playing on his weaknesses, he eventually convinced Crowley to step out of the mine and bring Scarlett with him.

"Where is she?" Crowley demanded. "Where is Ruby?"

"Two minutes," the negotiator said. "Just wait."

Cliff saw the car before the team.

The black Lincoln looked out of place traveling the winding mountain road. It pulled to a stop behind a CCPD squad car. A man wearing a suit emerged from the rear driver's side and strode confidently toward the hostage negotiator.

Crowley's father. He could be none other.

"What the hell is he doing here?" Crowley shouted.

"Your father wants to talk to you," the negotiator said.

Crowley wrapped an arm around Scarlett's neck. Forcing her to walk in front of him, he used her as a shield. Now that they were out in the open, Cliff had an unobstructed view—and he didn't like what he saw. Crowley's gun was shoved firmly against Scarlett's temple.

"Son." Crowley's father called out. The negotiator had given him the bullhorn. "Come down, now. Don't do anything rash. We can fix this."

Just as he'd had his attorneys find a tiny procedural error and get the charges dropped? Paid off the girls in college so they wouldn't testify? Turned a blind eye when his older son abused his younger one?

"Screw you, Dad."

"Listen, son. You need help."

Crowley continued to hurl obscenities and accusations at his father and demand that Ruby be brought to him. Cliff didn't like the way the young man sounded. He was unraveling at an alarming rate.

Perhaps Scarlett also sensed her captor's fragile mental state and was desperate to get away, for she suddenly started to struggle.

Ten feet separated Cliff and the two figures scuffling below him. He could jump. But what about Scarlett? If Crowley's gun went off...

There was little time left to act. It was now or not at all.

Cliff climbed swiftly to his feet. Beside him, Sarge also rose. God willing, the team would hold their fire.

Wait...wait...

The opportunity Cliff had been waiting for came. Scarlett broke free from Crowley and ran.

Leveling his gun at her, he screamed, "Bitch, I told you to stop."

Pulling his own weapon from his holster, Cliff leaped off the ledge. For a split second, he sailed through the air, Sarge right beside him. Then, the rocky ground came rushing up to meet them. Cliff landed with a bone crunching thud, tucked, rolled and rose. He tackled Crowley from behind, and they both went down.

Cliff didn't hold the advantage for long. Crowley was strong and hyped on whatever substance he'd taken. He flipped Cliff over onto his back and pinned him by the shoulders.

Cliff felt the cold barrel of Crowley's gun press into the soft flesh beneath his jaw.

"Drop it." Spittle sprayed from Crowley's mouth.

Cliff let his gun fall from his hand. He needed the precious seconds his surrender would buy him.

"You're a dead man," Crowley hissed in Cliff's ear.

"Not today." Cliff braced himself. "*Fass!*"

A low, lethal growl proceeded the attack. Crowley's head snapped back as if grabbed by a giant hand.

Not a hand. The jaws of a dog.

Sarge had a hold of Crowley between his neck and shoulder, and he wasn't letting go. Only the command to release from Cliff would accomplish that.

Crowley thrashed and screamed. Dropping his gun, he reached behind him for Sarge and grabbed handfuls of fur. Sarge wasn't fazed and held tight, his growls intensifying.

Cliff squirmed out from under Crowley and retrieved both guns. A glance to his left assured him Scarlett was all right. By then, the team was rushing up the hill. Only when Crowley was surrounded, and every available weapon pointed at him, did Cliff command Sarge to release Crowley.

"*Lass es. Hier.*"

The dog responded immediately and trotted over to where Cliff stood to receive his petting.

"Good boy."

Scarlett ran to Cliff and threw herself at him. "Thank you," she cried, her whole body trembling.

"Are you hurt?"

"I'm okay. I just want to go home."

"You will. But not till after you've been questioned."

"Do I have to?"

"I'll call ahead. Have Ruby meet you at the station."

One of the officers escorted Scarlett down the hill.

Crowley had been dragged upright and handcuffed. "What about my neck?" he demanded. "I'm bleeding."

"You'll receive proper care." Sheriff Eberhardt removed a handkerchief from his pocket and pressed it to Crowley's wound.

"That dog bit me. It's police brutality." He glared at Cliff. "I'm going to sue. You, the county, the whole freakin' state of Nevada."

"Good luck with that," Cliff said.

The deputies took Crowley away.

Sheriff Eberhardt came over to Cliff. "I assume we use your station to hold Crowley until transport arrives."

"It's all yours. We can question Scarlett next door in the community center." He didn't want her or Ruby anywhere near Crowley.

The sheriff glanced down at Sarge. "That's some partner you have."

"None better."

He shook Cliff's hand. "Nice working with you, Sheriff Dempsey. If you find yourself in my part of Washoe County, look me up."

"Count on it."

Cliff phoned Iva Lynn the moment he got to his SUV, breathing a sigh of relief when she told him Ruby was fine.

"You should know," Iva Lynn said, "only because you'll hear about it sooner or later, your aunt laid into Ruby. It was rough. She didn't pull any punches."

Not what he wanted to hear. "Great."

"The TV crew filmed it."

Even better. "Are they still in town?"

"Standing vigil outside the station. Along with three others. We've made national news."

Could his day get any worse? "Thanks, Iva Lynn."

"Your aunt wants to see you right away. I told her you'd be busy for a while."

Apparently, it could get worse.

"Bring Ruby to the community center. She'll have to be questioned along with her sister. And locate Will. Scarlett may be injured. Crowley definitely is. Have Will treat him first. If necessary, we'll take them to the clinic, but I'd rather avoid another media mob scene if possible."

"Right away." Iva Lynn hesitated before contacting the town's EMT. "You've made your father proud. Your grandfather, too, if he were alive."

Cliff's answer stuck in his throat. Not because of any sentimental flood of emotions, but because he didn't deserve Iva Lynn's praise.

He hadn't learned. He'd made the same mistake as before. Crossing the line. Letting his personal feelings cloud his judgment. It had almost cost Scarlett her life.

After Crowley was picked up and the sisters questioned, Cliff would meet with his aunt and the town council and accept whatever punishment they saw fit to dispense.

# Chapter Fourteen

Ruby didn't wait for Iva Lynn. She rushed toward the community-center door—and was instantly blocked by half a dozen reporters and just as many cameras.

"Ms. McPhee." A microphone was shoved in her face. Then another and another. "How do you feel now that Crowley has been apprehended?"

How did she feel? That was a dumb question.

"Whose idea was it to impersonate your sister, Scarlett? Yours or hers?"

"Is it true you and your sister are both dating Sheriff Dempsey?"

Ruby pushed the microphones away. "Please, I just want to see my sister."

Iva Lynn shot the closest reporter a look that could melt iron. "Ms. McPhee isn't answering any questions at this time."

Daunted, he stepped aside. Others followed, creating a path for Ruby. Once again, she'd underestimated the deputy.

At that moment, the mayor and members of the town council appeared, sparing Ruby. They became the instant target for a fresh barrage of questions.

"Mayor, how is this hostage situation going to affect the Mega Weekend of Weddings?"

"Are you going to cancel it?"

Oh, God. Ruby hadn't thought of that.

She and Iva Lynn weren't quite to the door when a commotion coming from the sheriff's station had the reporters scrambling away yet again.

Crowley, his wrists manacled and surrounded by law enforcement officers, was being escorted to an official vehicle. His father walked beside him, holding his suit jacket in front of his son's face to hide it.

The reporters converged on Crowley, only to be held back by a wall of police officers.

Ruby doubted he'd noticed her. Thank goodness for small favors. As he was pushed into the vehicle, his father dropped the jacket. Ruby caught a glimpse of Crowley and stared.

He barely resembled the handsome young man who had first come into the Century Casino's VIP Lounge. It wasn't just the ordeal from that morning affecting him. He had been on a downward spiral for months, and it wasn't over.

"Ruby?" Detective James jogged over from the station.

On impulse, she hugged him. "Thank you. For everything."

His surprise gave way to a wide smile. "I'm glad it's over. For good, this time."

"Me, too." Emotions threatened her composure. "How's Scarlett? Have you seen her?"

"She's fine. The town's EMT checked her out. A few cuts and bruises." He laughed. "Battle scars."

Will! Her boss, *Scarlett's* boss, was the EMT. He must be scratching his head in confusion. How could she face him again?

"This is all my fault. I shouldn't have come here." She was still stinging from the mayor's recent berating.

"Don't say that. Without you and your sister, we wouldn't have caught Crowley. And his next victim might have been less lucky."

"Yeah," Ruby reluctantly agreed.

The detective hitched his chin at the car with Crowley

in it. "I'd better get going. Make sure this guy gets booked correctly and with no mistakes. We aren't going through this a third time."

She couldn't wish for anything more.

"Take care, Detective."

Once he was on his way, she pushed open the door to the community center.

"Ruby!" Scarlett rushed to meet her halfway. The two held each other tight enough to crush ribs.

"You're okay." Tears filled her eyes and blurred her vision.

"I was so scared."

"I know, sweetie." She squeezed her sister even tighter. "If I could have changed places with you, I would have."

"How did you fight him off? I swear, I couldn't even move."

"He didn't have a gun that time."

When they finally pulled apart, it was to discover a roomful of eyes on them. Ruby realized this was the first time anyone other than Cliff had seen her and her sister together. Probably took some getting used to.

Several tables and folding chairs had been set up to accommodate all the people. Ruby recognized the mayor, Cliff's uncle and Will. Khaki and dark blue uniforms identified the Washoe deputies and the Carson City police officers. The others were strangers.

Cliff stood by one of the tables, his hip propped against it. She wanted to go to him—and would have if not for all "the eyes." Something told her a show of affection would generate the wrong kind of attention.

"Thank you for saving Scarlett." She smiled at him. Surely there was no harm in a simple smile. "Iva Lynn told me what you and Sarge did."

He nodded coolly. Obviously, he didn't want any attention, either.

Sarge had been lying on the floor next to Cliff and got up when Ruby entered the room. A sharp command from Cliff had kept him in place.

She didn't think a show of affection for Sarge would be taken wrong. Clapping her hands, she called, "Here, boy."

Sarge looked up at Cliff, who released him with a, *"Geh voraus."*

Sarge instantly bounded over. Ruby dropped to her knees and embraced him. "You're a good dog. I love you."

He made a wuffling sound she interpreted as, "I love you, too."

"Guess I'm going to have to learn to like dogs now. At least this one."

Ruby grinned up at her sister. "You do owe him a bone, I'd say."

Scarlett reached a tentative hand out and patted Sarge's head. "More like a dozen."

The dog licked her fingers.

Ruby snuck a peek at Cliff. His expression remained inscrutable, like the one he'd worn when she first knew him. Before he trusted her enough to lower his guard.

She stood. Not knowing what to do next, she stuffed her hands in her jeans pockets and waited. Sarge trotted back to Cliff and sat.

The door to the community center swung open, and a large man walked inside. Ruby had seen him among the law enforcement officials escorting Crowley to the car. From the way everyone instantly straightened, she assumed he was important.

"Who's that?" she whispered to Scarlett.

"I'm not sure. He was at the mine."

No wonder Cliff acted distantly. This was an intimidating audience.

"Can we leave now?" Scarlett asked no one in particular.

The large man in the khaki uniform answered. "We have

a few more questions for your sister, miss." He came over and introduced himself to Ruby. "I'm Sheriff Eberhardt. It's nice to meet you, Ms. McPhee."

He was courteous and pleasant. Ruby wasn't fooled for a second. This man meant business.

This interrogation would be like the one in Vegas after Crowley attacked her. She'd be treated like a criminal instead of a witness.

"What kind of questions, Sheriff?"

"I promise not to keep you long." The man gestured toward the metal chair where Scarlett had been sitting. "If you don't mind."

Ruby did mind. She glanced at Cliff, and he gave her a brief nod.

"Fine," she quipped, thinking that, until Crowley was behind bars, she would be answering a lot of questions. From the authorities. Reporters. Her boss. Coworkers. Family and friends. Might as well get used to it.

Another chair was brought over for Scarlett. Fortunately, the questioning didn't last long. Ruby had little to contribute to today's events, other than going over how she, Cliff and Scarlett agreed that Scarlett would watch the children.

At the mention of her and Cliff visiting the Gold Nugget to speak to Sam, "the eyes" darted furiously between the two of them. Ruby could practically hear the sound of wheels turning as everyone present put two and two together.

The temperature in the room jumped twenty degrees, and Ruby began to perspire. Cliff remained unaffected. How did he do it? Looking at him, no one would believe they were romantically involved.

Of course! *That* was the reason for his unusual behavior. He was protecting her reputation.

Her feelings for him grew even more.

Finally, Sheriff Eberhardt said, "You're free to go."

Holding hands, Ruby and Scarlett headed for the door. One of the officers hurried to open it for them.

Ruby paused, reluctant to leave without speaking to Cliff. But he hadn't spared her even a passing glance when she rose from her chair.

Iva Lynn followed behind them. "I'll drive you to the trailer."

A ride, Ruby hadn't thought of that. Scarlett's Jeep and the old pickup truck were both at the trailer and her car was still parked in the barn at the Gold Nugget.

"Okay, I guess."

"I'll bring your car by the trailer," Cliff said. "When we're done here."

Her heart would have leaped with joy if not for his flat delivery. She tried not to blow it out of proportion. This was just Cliff in sheriff mode.

"See you then." At Sarge's bark, she added, "He can come with me. I don't mind."

Cliff told Sarge to, *"Bleib."*

*Stay? Why?*

"His work guarding you is done."

The words stung worse than a slap to her face. Ruby's reply died as Scarlett dragged her outside.

She'd see Cliff later, and they'd talk. Ruby held on to that thought.

With Crowley apprehended, everything would return to normal. Maybe the mayor wouldn't hire her but surely Sam's offer of a job still held. One way or another, she and Cliff would move forward with their plans.

"COME IN, COME IN." Annie Wyler stood on the porch of the Gold Nugget ranch house, motioning them inside.

Scarlett went first, followed quickly by Ruby. Iva Lynn didn't hang around. She'd taken off the moment Annie appeared.

"Thank goodness that's over," Scarlett exclaimed.

Ruby's sentiments exactly. With Crowley gone, the reporters had turned again to Ruby and Scarlett for a story. Iva Lynn had lead them on a wild-goose chase through town. When they finally arrived at the trailer, it was to find several wily reporters lurking outside.

Iva Lynn changed tactics. A half hour later, they were at the Gold Nugget. Not home. But, fortunately, no reporters in sight.

Annie had hardly closed the door when Scarlett's cell phone rang.

"It's Demetri," she exclaimed with more delight than Ruby cared for. After a short conversation, she removed the phone from her ear and held it to her chest. "He saw the news. He's worried about me. Mind if I take this in private?"

"Use one of the upstairs bedrooms," Annie suggested.

Scarlett all but soared up the stairs.

"Can I get you something?" Annie asked. "Don't take this the wrong way, but you look awful."

"A glass of water maybe."

"Have you eaten?"

Ruby accompanied Annie to the kitchen. "I'm not hungry."

The other woman stopped suddenly and drew Ruby into an affectionate embrace. "I'm glad you and Scarlett are all right and that Crowley's caught."

Fighting back the tears was impossible. "It's been a rough day," Ruby said shakily.

"Sit. Take it easy." Annie guided her to the table.

Ruby slid into a seat and looked around. Like every time she returned to this kitchen, she was reminded of that first morning with Cliff.

She'd been terrified when he kissed her. Now, she missed his mouth on hers and longed for it with a desperation that cut deeper than she thought possible.

Rather than water, Annie brought over two steaming mugs of hot tea with lemon. Though Ruby hadn't thought of it, tea was exactly what she wanted.

"Thank you." She blew on the hot beverage before taking a sip.

"I'm sure you must hear this a lot, but seeing you and Scarlett together takes a little getting used to."

"We look a lot alike."

"Actually," Annie mused over her tea, "I was noticing how different you are. Not that I know either of you well. I think Cliff notices the differences, too."

"I hope he's okay." Ruby's glance strayed to the window over the sink, as if she could somehow shrink the miles separating them.

"Was he hurt in the rescue?"

"No. But he's acting funny."

Annie's expression turned pensive. "How so?"

"All business."

She dismissed Ruby's concerns with a chuckle. "That's Cliff for you. With both the CCPD and the Washoe County Sheriff's Department there, he's probably being his most professional."

Because of Talia, Ruby thought. Did Annie know Cliff's history?

"That reputation of his," Ruby said with a sigh.

"He does come from a long line of sheriffs. Folks here loved his father. And plenty of them remember his grandfather. They were both great men."

"So is Cliff. Today proved that."

"He's a shoo-in to win the election this fall."

A knock on the front door startled Ruby. After today, she would need a week to relax.

"Must be a guest. Be right back." Annie rose from the table and headed to the parlor.

Not a guest. Rather, a reporter. Ruby could hear the man's booming voice as it carried all the way from the front door.

"No, they're not here," Annie said sternly. "I'm going to have to insist you leave."

"Come on, ma'am. Give me a break."

"If you don't leave now, I'll call the sheriff."

The man required a bit more forceful coaxing from Annie before Ruby heard the door shut. She picked up her mug of tea with shaking fingers.

Scarlett entered the kitchen at the same time as Annie. Her demeanor was nothing short of glowing.

Ruby refrained from asking about the phone call until Annie had fixed Scarlett a cup of tea.

"I take it you're going back to San Diego?"

"Nope." Scarlett clasped her hands excitedly. "Demitri's coming here."

"Here?" Ruby sat back from the table.

"Not to stay. To help me pack my things," she added sheepishly.

Ah. Ruby understood. Scarlett and Demitri were back on.

"Please don't be mad at me."

She assumed Scarlett was addressing her. Instead, she was talking to Annie.

"I don't mean to give you and Sam such short notice. You've been good to me these past few months." Scarlett beamed at Ruby. "Now you can stay here and have my job."

"Absolutely," Annie concurred. "If that's what you want."

A few hours ago, Ruby would have pounced on the offer. Now, she wasn't sure if she should accept or reject it. Annie's earlier assurances about Cliff hadn't exactly quelled Ruby's fears.

"You can have the trailer once I've moved out," Scarlett continued. "Will won't mind, so long as he has a tenant."

Will. Another person Ruby and Scarlett had deceived.

He hadn't looked happy with her back at the community center. No one had.

"I should be out of there in a week."

A week. Where would Ruby stay in the meantime? With Cliff? She'd turned him down only this morning.

Her indecision must have shown for Annie said, "We have a vacancy here at the ranch."

The offer was kind. Like the woman herself and her entire family.

"Thanks. If you don't mind, I'd like to think about it." There was the casino owner's engagement party and her promise to Ernesto that she'd return to help out. "How soon will Demetri be here?"

"Tomorrow." Scarlett's glee had yet to diminish one iota.

"No rush, Ruby," Annie said. "Take your time."

"I need to talk to Cliff." More than talk. She needed to hold him and kiss him and hear him say his feelings for her hadn't changed.

"Let's call him." Annie popped up from the table and reached for her phone.

Had it been long enough?

"He said he'd bring my car by the trailer, and he hasn't shown up yet to get it. Not that he needs to now."

Annie wasn't listening to Ruby's ramblings. She was already placing the call. "Hmm. He's not answering." She dialed another number. "Let me try the mayor's office." After a moment, she announced, "It's going through."

Ruby waited, an uneasy dread filling her as the seconds ticked by.

"I see," Annie said. "No message. Thank you."

"What is it?" Ruby sat straighter.

"Cliff's in a meeting with his aunt and the entire town council." Annie's expression was grim. "They've left strict instructions not to be disturbed."

# Chapter Fifteen

Any other day, Cliff would have strode right into the main house at the Gold Nugget. Today, he knocked.

Ruby flung open the door. "You're here!"

The next instant, she was in his arms. He held her close, not wanting to let her go. Fearing when he did, he would likely never hold her again.

He'd made another costly mistake. Only this time, innocent people had been caught in the crossfire.

She found his mouth. Wrong as it was, Cliff returned the kiss. Later, when she wasn't so angry at him, she would remember this moment and, hopefully, his feelings for her.

When they broke apart, she smiled shyly and said, "Come inside."

"I can't stay."

"More business?"

"There is a lot of it. But that's not the reason." He swallowed. "We need to talk."

"I suppose we do." Her initial relief had been replaced with concern.

He didn't want to have this conversation standing in the doorway. "Let's take a walk."

She clasped his hand as they descended the porch steps. Had she done that before? It has always been him who reached for her.

He didn't dissuade her, though he really should. Intimate contact was only going to make matters worse when he delivered his news. But she clearly needed reassurance.

If only he could give it.

"I didn't have a chance to really thank you for saving Scarlett," she said. "It's all over the news. You're a hero."

Some might agree with her, but Cliff didn't feel like one. "Sarge deserves most of the credit."

"Did he come up with the idea of climbing that ledge?"

Cliff smiled despite himself. "I'm just glad Crowley's apprehended. And this time, the charges will stick."

"I doubt he'll get off because of a technicality."

"Not if Detective James has anything to do with it."

They reached the barn and went in to escape the warm, midafternoon sun. The ranch was mostly empty of guests. Cliff figured they were either in town, participating in the residual excitement, or hiding out in their cabins, afraid another stalker was in their midst.

According to his aunt, the second scenario was far more likely. To hear her talk, everyone on the planet now considered Sweetheart a hotbed for lowlifes and crime.

Her anger at him was understandable and deserved. She'd worked so hard to raise Sweetheart from the ashes—literally—only to have everything fall apart in a single day.

"Scarlett and Demitri have made up." Ruby sighed expansively.

"Are you surprised?"

"No. What I am surprised at is he's coming here."

"To live?"

"To help her pack and move to San Diego."

"She's quitting the ranch?"

"Told Annie an hour ago."

Without trying to appear obvious, Cliff led Ruby to her car parked next to the tractor. That way, when he broke her heart, she'd have the means for a quick getaway.

"I hope things work out for them," he said. Mostly because Scarlett's happiness would please Ruby.

"I give it three months. That's how long they lasted the last time."

"You know her better than I do."

"I was thinking of leaving for Vegas."

That announcement startled Cliff enough that he let go of her hand. Could it be possible she was going to make this easy for him?

"When?"

"Thursday at the latest. I've decided to cut Ernesto some slack."

Cliff remembered. "The engagement party."

"Yeah. And to give my official termination notice. Also grab some personal things and close up the condo." She leaned her back against the hood of the car. "I don't think I'm going to sell it yet."

"That's a good idea."

"I'll be back after the party."

"You don't have to hurry on my account."

She looked at him then. Closely. Intently. Realization dawned in her eyes. "Something's wrong?"

Much as he longed to touch her, he resisted. "Come back to Sweetheart, if that's what you really want."

"What do *you* want, Cliff?"

He spoke slowly, choosing his words carefully. "What I want isn't possible."

"I don't understand."

"Things have changed."

"Annie offered me Scarlett's old job. I'd still rather talk to your aunt first about a beverage manager position for the Mega Weekend of Weddings. If she'll listen to me."

"There isn't going to be any Weekend of Weddings."

Ruby frowned. "What?"

"Cancellations have been pouring in since the TV stations aired reports on Crowley. Couples are afraid to come here. As of thirty minutes ago, we're down to nineteen weddings."

She grew quiet. "Is that what your meeting with the town council was about?"

He paused. The memory was too fresh. Too painful. "They're considering revoking my appointment as sheriff."

"They can't do that!"

"Yes, they can. And they probably will. My position isn't official until after the election. Assuming I win. They're meeting again tomorrow to decide."

"But you're a Dempsey. A hero."

"Heroes don't put innocent people's lives in danger. My nieces and nephew could have been hurt. Scarlett is lucky to be alive."

"Nothing happened to any of them. Because of you."

"My aunt and the town council don't see it that way. I don't see it that way. I shouldn't have let Scarlett watch the kids. Not with Crowley on the loose, looking for you and roughing up your boss."

She pressed her hands to her cheeks. "You're wrong. This is my fault. And Scarlett's. Not yours. I shouldn't have come here. Your aunt told me that earlier, and she's right."

During their confrontation in town. The one that had also made the news and fueled his aunt's ire. Cliff's, too. At his aunt. She had no right to take her wrath at him out on Ruby.

"I'm sorry about that."

"It's okay," Ruby said. "She was scared. We were all scared. I'll speak to her. Clear this up."

"I wouldn't do that if I were you."

"She can't revoke *my* appointment!"

Another time, her remark might be funny. "My uncle's with her now. He has a knack for calming her down."

"I'll cancel my trip to Vegas," Ruby announced. "Stay here with you until this is all straightened out."

"Actually, I think you should stick to your original plan. Return to Vegas." He didn't add, "Just for the engagement party."

She searched his face, making him wish she wasn't so adept at reading him. "You're breaking up with me."

Had they ever really been together? He didn't think Ruby would appreciate the semantics. "It might be best if we kept our distance for a while."

"How long?"

"I don't know."

"Until after the town council decides on your appointment? Wait, that's tomorrow. After the engagement party? The Weekend of Weddings?" If there was one.

"Longer."

She pushed off the car. "Did your aunt put you up to this?"

"I'm not sure she even knows about us."

"So, this keeping our distance is entirely your idea?"

"Ruby, please try and understand."

"That your job is important to you? Oh, I get that." The faster she talked, the higher her voice rose. "And your position in this town. Your reputation. The tradition of passing the job down from one generation to the next. But let's be honest with each other, why don't we? Crowley showing up is my fault and you're punishing me for it by sending me away."

"I'm doing no such thing."

"Aren't you?" She glowered at him.

Cliff took a step back. "I screwed up before with Talia. Now, I've screwed up again. I let my feelings for you get in the way of me doing my job. I've spent the past two weeks protecting you from Crowley. And what do I do? I leave your sister alone with my nieces and nephew."

"You gave her strict instructions to go directly to the ranch. She didn't. If anyone's to blame, it's her."

"When has that woman ever done what she was told? Those kids were my responsibility, and I almost cost them their lives. Maeve is…"

"Mad at you?"

Cliff thought back to the terse phone conversation he had with his cousin. "Upset."

"You're letting your family make a bigger deal out of this than it is."

"It's a pretty big deal, Ruby."

She squeezed her eyes shut. "I know, I'm sorry. I didn't mean to imply your nieces and nephew aren't important. I just don't see what this whole thing has to do with us."

"I wanted to spend more time with you."

"Wanted?"

"This morning. The reason I agreed to let Scarlett watch the kids was because I wanted to spend time with you."

"Is that so awful?"

"Yes, when it affects my judgment."

"You saved Scarlett. Surely that cancels out any trivial mistake."

"That's not how it works. I'm charged with protecting this town and everyone in it. I can't make mistakes. Large or trivial."

"Are you going to forego personal relationships your entire career because caring for someone might affect your judgment?" She visibly fought for composure. "That's pretty extreme, Cliff. Your father didn't do it. Neither did the rest of the Dempsey sheriffs. Why should you?"

"I don't have the answer."

"You dated my sister, for crying out loud."

"It wasn't the same. I didn't—" He stopped himself before saying too much.

"What?" she insisted.

"The relationship wasn't ever going to go anywhere."

"It doesn't look like ours is, either." Her mouth trembled in an effort not to cry.

He couldn't let her hurt deter him. "The town's in trouble. I have to do my best to fix it."

"And not screw up a second law enforcement career."

Her remark struck him like a missile straight to the chest. Recovering took a moment.

"I have a responsibility, an obligation to give this town, its citizens, my best service."

"And you did today. You apprehended a criminal and saved a life. *Service* doesn't get any better."

Not according to his aunt. "Sweetheart depends on tourists. People who come here need to know they're safe and their families are safe. I can't protect them if I'm distracted."

"Is that what I am? A distraction?"

Hurting her had been inevitable. He just hadn't realized how much her reaction would hurt him.

"You're not. You mean more to me than anyone else.

"Then prove it."

She should be able to expect that from a man who proclaimed to care for her. "I can't go against my aunt and the town council. Not while the future of Sweetheart is at stake."

"Never mind, Cliff." Ruby dug her keys out of her pocket and opened the car door. "You obviously don't care about me, or I wouldn't have to expend this much effort convincing you what we have is worth fighting for."

"Please, Ruby. Don't."

"Don't what? Leave? You just told me not to hurry back on your account. Don't leave mad? What else did you expect? Don't return to Sweetheart? That can be arranged."

She was probably too busy mentally slicing him into a hundred thousand pieces to notice the door to the barn wasn't open.

Cliff could either walk over and open the door or stop

her from going. The choice should be easy. Losing Ruby would tear him in two. In the end, he did what he had to.

Sliding the wooden bar across the door, he flung it open and stood to the side.

Ruby rammed the car in reverse and backed out. Dirt and debris from the soft barn floor spit out from beneath her tires and showered the bottom half of Cliff's pants.

She couldn't have made her goodbye any clearer.

He didn't watch her drive away. It was too hard. Instead, he closed the door and wandered through the barn, stopping briefly at the stalls. The old mare and pony stuck their heads out and nickered for attention. Cliff absently stroked one soft muzzle, then the other.

Difficult as it would be for both him and Ruby, he'd made the right decision. Like rebreaking a bone that wasn't healing correctly. Hurt like hell at first, but eventually it would mend and be good as new. Maybe even stronger.

Yeah, just continue telling himself stupid analogies like that one for the next fifty years, and eventually he'd feel better.

Cliff leaned his forearms on the pony's stall door and did something he hadn't when the Reno drug raid went to hell in a hand basket. Something he hadn't done since he was thirteen and got punched in the nose by an older boy at school.

He fought back tears.

TWO-AND-A-HALF WEEKS. The amount of time Ruby had been gone. Yet it felt to Ruby as if she'd been away a lifetime. Everything was strange and surreal. The city. Her condo. The casino. Even now, the serving station in the VIP lounge, a place she'd stood countless times overseeing the staff, looked different. As if someone had redecorated in her brief absence. Only no one had.

Where were the mountains? The tall ponderosa pines?

The quaint storefronts and charming homes? The down-home friendliness?

Did falling in love change a person's perspective? If not, then having one's heart broken certainly did.

She hadn't fully admitted to herself that she loved Cliff until reaching the outskirts of Sweetheart. It had taken every ounce of willpower she possessed not to turn her car around.

She might have done it was there any chance he'd change his mind about them. That uncompromising expression he'd worn when she'd peeled away erased all doubt.

Ruby would carry the memory with her for the rest of her life. Cliff cared for her, she was sure of it. *Had* cared for her. But not enough to stand up to his family and risk that damn reputation he was always so worried about.

Would she do the same in his shoes? Jeopardize her job and her relationship with her family?

Before going to Sweetheart, the answer would have been a resounding yes. After watching the news, she had her doubts.

Everywhere she went, headlines screamed and TVs and radios blasted the latest update. She couldn't stroll through the casino without a TV in one of the bars or lobbies reaching her ears. Was nothing else newsworthy?

Then there were her friends and coworkers, all of them eager to fill her in on what they'd heard or ask probing questions about Crowley and her sister's abduction. If not for the casino's top-notch security staff, Ruby wouldn't have made it past the reporters waiting in the lobby.

According to the latest interview with Mayor Dempsey, the Mega Weekend of Weddings had been cancelled. She'd expressed grave concern about the town's prospects to recover in the wake of another disaster.

Ruby's broken heart cried a little.

Late-night talks with herself and sympathy from friends hadn't made a difference. Fine, she wasn't to blame for

Crowley's actions. He's the one who decided to get ramped up on his mother's cocaine, drive to Sweetheart and abduct Ruby.

But he wouldn't have come to Sweetheart if not for her, as Mayor Dempsey had vehemently pointed out.

Ruby sighed. It always came back to her. As did the terrible breakup with Cliff.

That was also preventable. She should have stuck to her guns in the beginning and not gotten involved with him until Crowley was no longer a threat. But she hadn't.

Still, if he loved her...

Except he didn't. He hadn't even called to check up on her. She needed to toss that disposal phone instead of hanging on to it.

"*Chica!* Why the long face?"

She felt a comforting hand on her shoulder.

Ernesto. Again. He'd been hovering over her like a mother hen since her return. Truth be told, she loved him for it.

Tucking the notepad and pen she'd been holding into her uniform pocket, she faced him. Among her other duties tonight, she was personally serving the casino owner's table. He and his guests would want for nothing.

"I'm fine," she told Ernesto.

"Admit it." He winked knowingly. "You were thinking about him."

Ernesto was the only person she'd told about Cliff. Unburdening herself hadn't lightened her emotional load. Ruby was still miserable.

"It's over. I need to move on."

He pulled her close, and Ruby caught a whiff of his trademark flowery cologne. Her boss was nothing if not flamboyant, from his neon-colored shirts to his Italian leather shoes. On him, in his job, the style worked. He was an extremely good manager, well-liked by the customers and highly regarded by the employees.

"The heart needs time to heal," he advised Ruby. "Don't rush. However, if you change your mind, there's a new guy on the floor. A blackjack dealer. Very much your type."

She had to laugh at that. "I'm not dating for a while."

Ernesto tsk'd sympathetically. "Of course you aren't. Not after your experience with that dreadful man Crowley." He laid a hand on his chest. "It's my fault. I should have taken your complaints more seriously."

How many people were going to claim responsibility for what happened? Her. Cliff. Scarlett and Ernesto. Were Crowley's parents feeling the least bit guilty? The rookie cop who'd made the mistake during Crowley's first arrest?

She bit back a rush of anger. Crowley alone was to blame. "It's all right, Ernesto. Don't worry."

"But I do, *chica*. I want the old Ruby back."

In the large room, the casino owner's engagement party was in full swing. The VIP lounge could easily hold two hundred, and at least that many were here tonight. More were expected.

Considering the noise and activity level, it was a wonder Ruby and Ernesto were able to hold a conversation. Nearby, the wait staff scurried to and fro, their trays laden with champagne glasses and hors d'oeuvres.

"I should have insisted Crowley be banned from the casino the first time he gave you trouble." Ernesto rolled his eyes. "Mr. Xavier wouldn't hear of it."

"Crowley's father is a very influential politician," Ruby said. "Mr. Xavier didn't have a choice."

"Bah!" Ernesto dismissed her words with a wave.

"You're wrong, I did have a choice."

Ruby and Ernesto spun in unison, their mouths hanging open.

Mr. Xavier stood in front of them, having come in via the private entrance. She and Ernesto had been too occupied to notice.

Ruby's cheeks warmed.

"I apologize, sir." Ernesto hung his head.

"Don't. Either of you." Mr. Xavier strode forward. "It's me who owes you and Ruby an apology."

In his mid-fifties, the man was fit, handsome, successful and wealthy. His fiancée, the center of attention at the party, was ten years his junior but looked twenty.

They were a striking couple and, from all accounts, deeply in love. Ruby wished them the happiness that had eluded her and Cliff.

Mr. Xavier came over and took Ruby's hands in his, startling her. Though always kind, he maintained a professional distance from the employees. A point he and Cliff would agree on.

"I was too concerned with how banning young Crowley would affect business when I should have been concerned about the welfare of one of my best people."

Another person taking responsibility for Crowley's actions. When would this stop?

"His father is a good customer," she said. "With a lot of friends in high places."

*Was* a good customer. Crowley senior hadn't visited the casino since his son's arrest. Probably, like Ruby, he was avoiding the reporters.

"I'm sorry about the adverse attention this has brought the casino," she said.

"Are you joking?" His raucous laughter momentarily drowned out the noise. "Business is booming."

Ruby thought his celebrity fiancée might have more to do with it.

"If there's anything you need," Mr. Xavier continued. "Anything I can do, just let me know."

"Thank you, sir, but I'm fine."

A cheer rose from Mr. Xavier's table. The celebration was escalating.

So much excitement for one wedding, Ruby thought. Sweetheart used to host hundreds a year. Now, they couldn't give one away. Because a cloud of fear hung over the town.

"If you'll excuse me." Mr. Xavier smiled and started to walk away. "My bride-to-be and my guests are waiting for me."

*One wedding...*

Ruby surprised herself by calling out, "Mr. Xavier."

He stopped, his expression expectant. "Yes."

"There *is* something you can do."

"Of course." A tiny hint of impatience tinged his voice.

"Not for me, actually. But for some people who are very important to me."

"What's that?"

She gathered her courage, still not quite believing what she was about to say. "Have you and Ms. Lilly decided on the destination for your wedding?"

"Not yet. We're hoping to avoid the crowds and paparazzi."

She had just the place for them.

"What about Sweetheart? It's really beautiful. Incredible scenery. And small. Hardly any tourists." *Thanks to her.*

"Sweetheart? Where you and Crowley—"

"Before you say no, think about it. The town is dying. Their big wedding event was cancelled and people are staying away in droves. The town could really use a boost."

"We were thinking of a small, private wedding. Someplace secluded."

Ruby climbed further out onto the limb. "What if your wedding wasn't so small and not so private?"

He actually appeared to consider her idea.

*Please, please, please.*

"I don't know." He shook his head.

"It could change a lot of lives. The increase in business could carry the town for months. And generate publicity for the casino. You said yourself, if there was anything you could do."

"It's true. I should have taken your concerns about Crowley more seriously..." He shook his head again, more vehemently. "Sweetheart isn't what we had in mind."

Ernesto, bless his heart, came to Ruby's aid. "The casino could cater the event. Transport everything you would need. Food. Drinks. Wait staff. Decorations. Security."

"What the casino can't transport, Sweetheart will provide," Ruby added. "They've been in the wedding industry for over a century. Literally."

At that moment, Mr. Xavier's fiancée appeared. "There you are." She glided over to him, tall, graceful and radiant. Linking her arm in his, she asked, "Am I interrupting a meeting?"

"Ruby here has come up with a suggestion for our wedding destination."

"Oh?" She turned her lovely smile on Ruby. "Where's that?"

"Sweetheart," Mr. Xavier answered. "She's suggesting instead of a small affair, we pull out all the stops. The town is struggling. A big, splashy celebrity wedding might—"

"I think it's a great idea!"

"You do?" Mr. Xavier's thick brows rose with surprise.

"My grandparents eloped to Sweetheart when they were just teenagers. They were married sixty-four years. Sixty-four years," she repeated in awe. "My parents took us on a family vacation there when we were young. It's beautiful. And the chapel—" She looked at Ruby. "Is the chapel still there? Tell me it didn't burn down."

Ruby had difficulty containing her excitement. "It's still there."

Ms. Lilly brightened. "It's settled then."

"Are you sure?"

"Darling, if we can help the town, then we should do it.

Besides," she pinched his cheek, "we don't have to wait. We can get married in a few weeks."

"All right." He kissed her soundly on the lips. "Pick a date."

"Is three weeks from today too soon?"

"Can you be ready by then?"

"I'm ready to marry you today." She kissed him back.

Ruby could have fainted with relief. Sweetheart may not be hosting a hundred small weddings in one weekend, but they were about to host one of the biggest celebrity weddings of the year.

"It seems you and Ernesto have a job ahead of you."

"A job, sir?" Ruby exchanged glances with her boss.

"Putting on a wedding. We can't do this without my best manager and assistant manager."

"Sir, I…" Ruby faltered, and her voice deserted her. Cliff was in Sweetheart.

"You can't say no."

He was right. She couldn't. Not after he and his fiancée had agreed to her idea.

"It would be my pleasure."

She would just have to find a way to avoid running into Cliff while she was there.

It shouldn't be too hard. They'd both be busy. Her with the wedding and Cliff with…what? Was he still sheriff? Scarlett said she hadn't seen him around. Then again, she'd been preoccupied with moving to San Diego.

The remainder of the night was a whirlwind for Ruby. Yet, all she could think about was returning to Sweetheart and avoiding Cliff…

…when she wasn't thinking about how *not* to avoid Cliff.

## Chapter Sixteen

TV reporters had invaded Sweetheart once again. This time, the reason was a good one. The casino owner's wedding to his celebrity fiancée.

Cliff peered out the sheriff station's small window, his view partially obstructed by the security bars. He wasn't looking for Ruby. And if he repeated that enough times, he might eventually believe it. She was here, according to Iva Lynn's latest communication.

For the moment, his deputy was overseeing security, along with a team from the casino. In a few hours, when guests started arriving, dozens of personal bodyguards belonging to the Hollywood stars would be added to the mix. At some point very soon, Cliff would need to make another appearance.

He measured the distance separating him and Ruby in footsteps. Less than a hundred. She was right next door in the community center, the only building in town large enough to accommodate a reception of hundreds and with a kitchen.

Already, the parking lot was a mob scene. Vehicles of all manner and make were jammed together, from limos to vans to refrigerated trucks. Fans, tourists and locals lined up behind the temporary barricades, hoping to catch sight of the many rich and famous scheduled to arrive. Security guards prevented them from crossing the barricade and getting too close.

Conversely, only a few dozen close friends and family members would be attending the ceremony in the small chapel. Cliff had just come from there. The entire street was blocked. Sheriff Eberhardt had dispatched several teams of deputies to assist Cliff.

He couldn't ever remember a day like this one.

Sarge gave a lonely woof from his place by the desk. The dog must somehow sense Ruby was near.

Cliff left the window, giving Sarge a sympathetic pat in passing. "Later I'll have Iva Lynn take you over to see her."

Or, *he* could.

What would she do? Smile and greet him warmly? Be coolly polite? Deliver the verbal lambasting he deserved?

She hadn't made any attempt to contact him in the month since they'd last seen each other. Not to tell him about the casino owner's wedding—Mr. Xavier's personal assistant had been the one to call the mayor—or to let him know she would be among the casino staff working the event. He'd seen her name on a list provided to his aunt.

That had been a shock. And, yet, it hadn't. He tried not to read more into her appearance than there was. Clearly she hadn't used the wedding as an excuse to see him.

What did he expect after the way he'd treated her?

The door to the station opened. For a brief moment, Cliff's heart skidded to a stop. It resumed normal rhythm upon seeing his aunt.

"Am I interrupting?" she asked.

"Come on in."

They were getting along better these days than they had immediately following Scarlett's abduction and Crowley's arrest. The town council had voted unanimously not to revoke Cliff's appointment. He had received a severe reprimand, however. A personal one. From his aunt and cousin. Everyone else thought, like Ruby did, that Cliff was a hero.

He still didn't feel like one, even after the glowing accounts of his actions reported by the various news media. The county was giving him and Sarge a commendation.

It changed nothing. In his mind, he'd still made a terrible mistake that could have cost four lives.

"What can I do for you?" he asked his aunt.

"Come to the wedding and reception."

"Iva Lynn and the Washoe deputies are handling things."

"I want you there, Cliff. As a representative of the town." She moved further into the station, closing the door behind her. "You're the reason Mr. Xavier's having us host his wedding."

"Ruby is. Not me."

Xavier's personal assistant had told them Ruby suggested the wedding be held in Sweetheart. It was, he realized, exactly something she'd do. Hard as it might be for her to return, she thought first of others.

"I was wrong," his aunt said.

They'd been through this before. "You don't need to apologize again."

"You're right, I don't and I won't. Everybody's fine. Maeve and the kids are in trauma counseling and doing great. She doesn't blame you. If fact, she's proud of you. So am I. What you did took real courage. With all the publicity and revenues from this weekend, the town will soon be back on its feet."

"Then why the visit, Aunt Hilda?"

"I'm sorry I didn't realize the extent of your feelings for Ruby before I lashed out at her." She smiled crookedly. "It sounds strange saying her name. I still think of her as Scarlett."

"Anything Ruby and I had is over."

"Really? Is that why you're hiding out here and letting your deputy do your job?"

"I came back to make some calls."

His aunt harrumphed. "You can't avoid her all weekend. You shouldn't avoid her."

"I doubt she wants to see me."

"Maybe she's just as afraid to take the first step as you."

"I'm not afraid."

"Yeah? How about stubborn? You think I don't know how the Dempsey men operate?"

"You're butting in where you don't belong."

"That's what families do, Cliff." She reached up and brushed his hair as if he were a small boy. "I've made a lot of mistakes in my life. Coming between you and Ruby is one of my biggest."

"There was nothing to come between."

"Do you love her?"

More than he'd thought it was possible to love anyone. "No."

"You always were a terrible liar."

Cliff had had just about enough and sat at his desk.

She didn't take the hint. Bracing her hands on the desk in front of him, she said, "Don't let this opportunity pass without talking to her. Even if it's just to thank her for all she's done."

"I'll think about it."

"She'd be good for you, Cliff. And for this town. Folks appreciate what she's done for them. You do have an election coming up," she added and straightened.

"Are you suggesting I reconcile with Ruby just to win votes?"

"I'm suggesting you reconcile with her because you're crazily, madly in love. Votes are a perk."

His aunt wasn't joking. She took politics very seriously. Until Scarlett's abduction, Cliff had been running unopposed. A week later, an opportunist on the town council declared his candidacy.

"I can't afford another mistake. My career is too important to me." Cliff desperately wanted this conversation to be at an end.

"It's water under the bridge. Let it go. Crowley's accepted a plea and is going to serve time. Our family is safe. The town is making a comeback."

And the woman he was crazily, madly in love with was fewer than a hundred footsteps away.

"All that doesn't change the fact I made a potentially costly error in judgment."

"You know, I'm getting tired of hearing you say that. Okay, you screwed up. Well, you're about to screw up again. Worse this time."

"She doesn't want to see me."

"I could order you to come to the wedding."

He almost wished she would but said nothing.

"Have it your way." His aunt finally left, slamming the door behind her.

Cliff didn't like being left alone with his thoughts.

In Reno, he'd quit the force, citing his father's retirement and a family tradition to uphold. In truth, he'd left rather than face his problems head on.

He was doing the same thing now. Only instead of leaving, he was holed up in the station. Same difference.

No, not the same. This time, he wasn't just walking away from a career, he was walking away from the love of a lifetime.

Sarge whimpered. He evidently agreed with Cliff.

The door opened again. Cliff braced himself. Only it wasn't his aunt returning.

"We need you." Sam stood on the threshold, one hand on the doorknob.

What was he doing here? "I already told my aunt, I'm not—"

"There's been a theft. Someone stole the bride's wedding ring."

CLIFF ADJUSTED HIS cowboy hat as he entered the community center, fitting it more snugly on his head. Behind him, Iva Lynn shut the double doors and locked them, then stood guard.

There were easily four dozen people in the room, including the groom. He didn't look too distressed for being the victim of a crime.

Everyone save Iva Lynn, Xavier, Cliff's aunt and Sam stood along the far wall. Cliff identified them by their uniforms. Cooks, servers, bar staff and security. One man and one woman wore suits. Xavier's personal assistants, Cliff surmised. It would be far worse if the guests were present.

He immediately spotted Ruby. She stood seven in from the right. He hadn't seen her in her uniform before. The short skirt and high heels looked good on her. *Great* on her. He still liked her better in a pair of snug jeans.

Their glances met. He waited for her to look away. She didn't. Neither did he.

He wished now he'd taken his aunt's advice and spoken to her. If only to inquire how she was doing. Then, he wouldn't be forced to have everyone in the room witness his reaction.

Schooling his features, he approached Xavier. "I'm Sheriff Dempsey. I understand your ring was stolen."

"My fiancée's gold wedding band."

"When did you last have it?"

He scratched his head. "Half an hour ago. Maybe twenty minutes."

"Where was it then?"

"In my pocket." He patted the front of his tuxedo. "I

haven't let it out of my possession all morning. I went to give the ring to my best man, and it was gone."

"Has anyone left the room in that time?"

"I couldn't count how many. The staff has been coming and going since I got here."

That would make it harder. "Are all the staff accounted for?"

Xavier's female assistant hurriedly consulted a clipboard, then scanned the room, her mouth silently moving as she counted.

This was taking a while, so Cliff continued questioning Xavier.

"Has anyone had access to your tuxedo?"

"No."

"Did you take off your jacket at any point?"

Xavier shook his head.

A pickpocket? Cliff weighed the possibilities. "Is there anyone in the room you don't know?"

"I know everyone. They all work for me."

"Might any of them carry a grudge against you?"

He laughed then. "I'm their employer. They probably all carry a grudge."

"All accounted for," the assistant declared.

Something about the situation struck Cliff as off. In addition to Xavier's unconcerned behavior, Sam was acting suspicious. Iva Lynn, too. She and his aunt kept exchanging glances.

"I'll need to question everyone."

"Perhaps you should have them empty their pockets," Xavier said. "Wouldn't that be quicker?"

"In due time."

Cliff's aunt stepped forward. "Will all of you please empty your pockets."

"Mayor." Cliff warned. He wouldn't tolerate her interfering with an official investigation.

Unfortunately, no one else in the room was aware of that. One by one, they did as his aunt instructed. Before Cliff could stop him, the casino owner started walking down the line, examining the contents in everyone's hands.

Cliff was losing control. Not a state he could tolerate. He went after the man. "Mr. Xavier. If you don't mind—"

"There it is!" the man exclaimed. He'd stopped in front of Ruby.

*She'd* stolen his ring?

"This?" She held up a tiny manila envelope.

"That's my bride's ring."

Her face blanched. "Mr. Xavier, you gave this to me. Asked me to hold it for you."

"I did not!"

"Sir, you did. I was standing by the kitchen entrance, and you gave me the envelope with strict instructions to hold on to it."

"Didn't you wonder what was in the envelope?" Cliff asked.

She turned a blank expression on him. "He's my boss."

Xavier took the envelope from her, tore it open and shook the ring into his palm. "Obviously, there's been a mistake." He appealed to Cliff, a smile spreading across his face. "You two talk. I'm sure you can sort it out." He gestured toward the door, which Iva Lynn opened as if on cue. "Let's give them some privacy, shall we?"

The room promptly emptied. Sam tipped his hat as he left. His aunt winked.

In a flash, it all became crystal clear.

"Cliff," Ruby protested, her voice breaking. "I didn't steal the ring."

"I know. We've been set up."

"Set up?"

Their voices echoed loudly in the now empty room.

Cliff lowered his. "I doubt Xavier was the mastermind,

but he was a willing participant. My money's on my aunt and Iva Lynn."

"I don't understand."

"Matchmaking is something of a town tradition."

"I'm sorry." She averted her eyes.

He caught her chin and tipped her face toward him. "I'm not, Ruby. I should have talked to you earlier."

"It's all right."

"I've been a jerk."

"I understand why you did what you did."

"Then maybe you can explain it to me because I can't figure out how I could have let you drive away that day."

"You were scared."

She'd always been able to read him. "I was. It's been a while since I've felt so strongly about a woman."

"And the last one betrayed you."

He thought the flicker shining in her eyes might be hope. The emotion was certainly growing inside him by leaps and bounds.

"I want to get to know you. The real Ruby McPhee. Not someone pretending to be her sister." He took her hand, enjoying the feel of her soft fingers in his. "And I want you to get to know me. The sheriff of Sweetheart. Not the former Reno police officer escaping his past."

"Vegas is a long drive."

"Sarge will keep me company."

"What about the election? Won't you need to campaign?"

"I'm going to win, Ruby. The election and your heart. If you'll give me half a chance."

Her answer was to stand on her tiptoes and plant a light kiss on his lips. "Sheriff Dempsey, let me introduce myself. I'm Ruby McPhee."

"Nice to meet you, Ms. McPhee. You don't happen to be free for dinner anytime soon?"

She grinned. "As it so happens, my schedule is wide open."

Cliff swept her into his arms and kissed her with a hunger that had been building this last, long month. God, he's missed her.

Vegas? He'd drive to Maine and back for this. Twice.

He would have continued kissing her indefinitely if the doors didn't all at once swing open with a resounding bang.

They heard a "Sarge, come back here," before being body slammed by a hundred-and-twenty pounds of excited German shepherd. He'd have knocked Ruby to the floor if Cliff wasn't there to catch her.

She knelt and hugged Sarge by the neck as he showered her with kisses. "I missed you, too, boy."

People began streaming back into the community center. No one mentioned the recovered wedding ring.

Xavier strode over to them. "I take it all's been resolved satisfactorily."

Ruby's cheeks bloomed a pretty pink. "Yes, sir."

"Good job, Sheriff." He shook Cliff's hand. "I'm impressed."

Cliff nodded.

Ruby touched his arm. "I need to get back to work." She checked her watch. "The reception's in four hours."

"I'm afraid that's not possible," Xavier said, suddenly sobering.

"The wedding's off!" She gave a small gasp.

"Absolutely not. But you can't return to work."

"Why?"

"You're fired."

"I didn't take the—"

Cliff stepped forward, ready to defend her.

Xavier chuckled. "You're fired because you can't possibly hold down a job in Vegas while the man you love is here in Sweetheart." He placed an arm around Ruby's shoulders.

"And for your severance pay, I'm giving you and the sheriff the biggest wedding this town has seen. Next to mine, of course."

"I—I can't…"

"You can, Ruby."

She turned to Cliff. "What should I do?"

"Whatever you want, honey. You're choice." Having just found her again, he had no intentions of scaring her away by putting too much pressure on her.

She chewed her lower lip, then said determinedly, "No, Mr. Xavier, I won't let you fire me."

Cliff was disappointed, but he didn't show it.

"Not until after the reception." She smiled at her boss. "I made a promise."

"Good decision." He gave her a peck on the cheek.

She searched out Sam. "Do you think I can have my old job back? Scarlett's old job, I mean."

"I have a better one for you," Cliff's aunt interrupted Sam before he could answer.

"Then, I guess I've never been so glad to be fired before."

Cliff hardly heard the ruckus that erupted as he lost himself in the thrill of kissing Ruby.

# Epilogue

Ruby's hands trembled, causing the flowers in the bouquet she held to flutter. Were all brides this nervous?

She looked over at Cliff, tall and handsome in his dress uniform. Perspiration beaded above his brows, and his breathing was shallow. Grooms, too, apparently got nervous.

He gave her a reassuring smile, his blue eyes crinkling at the corners. Like that, her jitters dissipated. She was about to become Mrs. Cliff Dempsey, wife of the sheriff of Sweetheart.

She was also about to become a mother and Cliff a father. Not for seven-and-three-quarter months. Cliff didn't know it yet. She was saving the news for their honeymoon. A week in a resort at Lake Tahoe.

Ruby McPhee—make that Dempsey—a mother-to-be. And actually looking forward to it. She'd learned a lot from Erin, Ellie and Evan this past year. Most importantly, that she wasn't bad with kids at all. She just might be able to successfully raise one or two of her own.

Cliff would help. The wannabe family man's fondest wish was finally becoming a reality. She gazed at him again, her love so strong, so powerful, she thought it might just spill out of her.

The two of them stood side by side in the mayor's office.

Despite Mr. Xavier's generous offer to pay for their wedding, they'd chosen to have a small, private ceremony officiated by Cliff's aunt and witnessed by Scarlett and Sam.

They weren't the only ones in attendance. Demitri, of course, was there. Unbelievably, his and Scarlett's last reconciliation had stuck. They were soon off to Australia and the Great Barrier Reef for three months.

Maeve and the children, too, as well as Annie. Ruby wouldn't have been able to pull off even this small service without the other women's help. She'd miss Scarlett terribly, but Maeve and Annie's friendship would help fill the void. The two had even traveled with Ruby on her last trip to Vegas when she'd purchased her wedding dress and finalized the sale of her condo.

Cliff's parents had flown in for the wedding. Ruby had gotten to know them over this past year and considered herself the luckiest bride ever to have such delightful in-laws. Her parents arrived that morning—separately—and were making an effort to get along for Ruby's sake, something she greatly appreciated.

The mayor delivered a short, deeply moving speech before having Ruby and Cliff recite their vows. "Do you have the rings?" she asked.

Erin and Ellie pushed Sarge forward. "Go on," they chimed.

Until then, the dog been sitting quietly. At the girls' prodding, he hop-walked toward Ruby and Cliff. The frilly white pillow strapped to his back bobbed back and forth. Two gold rings were tied to the pillow, joined with a single silk ribbon.

Cliff patted Sarge and untied the rings, giving his to Ruby and holding on to hers. His job done, Sarge lay down at their feet. Resting his head on his paws, he made a woofing sound. His way of saying, "Well, it took you long enough."

After the "with this ring I thee wed" parts were done, the mayor announced, "You may kiss your bride."

Cliff did. Thoroughly enough to curl Ruby's toes inside her dressy white heels. She certainly had a lot to look forward to over the next fifty or sixty years.

He held her close a moment longer and whispered in her ear, "I love you, Ruby. I have from the first moment I saw you."

"I love you, too." She didn't think she'd ever get tired of telling him that.

They turned to accept the congratulations of their family and friends. Sarge howled, something Ruby had never heard him do. Erin, Ellie and Evan rushed over to dispense hugs. The men made a show of shaking hands and clapping shoulders. More congratulations followed.

The biggest hug came from the mayor. "Welcome to the family," she gushed.

"Thank you for everything."

"Let's eat," Ellie announced.

"Who's hungry?" Cliff asked.

"I want cake," Evan said. He'd grown a lot in the last year, as had his vocabulary.

Ruby ruffled his hair. "Well, young man, we just happen to have cake."

The reception would include a few more people than the service. About a hundred. Ruby had overseen the preparations herself. All in a day's work for Sweetheart's catering coordinator.

After Mr. Xavier's extravagant wedding last summer, couples had started returning to Sweetheart. Slowly at first, then in droves. Tourists, too. The site where Cliff had saved Scarlett and apprehended Crowley was the town's newest attraction.

Ruby didn't care what brought people to Sweetheart as long as they came. Except for Crowley. She wanted him to stay far, far away. Even with the plea he accepted, it would be several years before he was eligible for parole. Ruby felt certain they'd seen the last of him.

Sam opened the door to the mayor's office. It was only a few yards to the community center where the reception was being held.

Cliff held Ruby's hand as they stepped outside into the bright afternoon sunlight—and were promptly greeted by hundreds of people.

Where had they all come from? And when? They filled the parking lot and overflowed into the street.

"Wh-what's going on?" she stammered.

A cheer rose up, filling the air.

The mayor put her mouth to Ruby's ear. "You didn't think Sweetheart's favorite couple was getting married without half the town showing up."

Ruby couldn't believe it. She shared a joyful smile with Cliff.

"Better give them what they came for," the mayor hollered above the noise.

Cliff gathered Ruby into to his arms.

"Kiss her, kiss her," the crowd chanted.

Cliff obliged, and the cheering escalated.

Arm in arm, they waved to the crowd as they walked to the community center where the celebration continued long into the night, as wondrous and magical as the town in which they lived.

\* \* \* \* \*